"I had a strange dream," said the hetman, "a drunken shaman's dream. There was a red sun in the sky, a sun which was like a giant eye. An immense lid covered it, which winked slowly, with a sort of malice. A great tear fell on the earth, a red tear, hot and burning. It looked like lava, or blood. And this red, hot, burning tear—covered the earth, slowly wearing a path toward me. I was standing on a little mound of dry grass and I couldn't move ... In the burning sky the strange eye gathered another droplet ...

"Then there was a rumbling, a long sound like voices, and I saw a band of black riders come down from the sky and ride straight toward me, as if the bloody tear had opened the way for them. A burning pain reached my feet, a grip along my legs. The black riders were brandishing weapons that glittered in the night. ..."

By Daniel Walther:

THE BOOK OF SHAI

SHAI'S DESTINY

Daniel Walther

Translated by C.J. Cherryh

DAW BOOKS, INC.
DONALD A. WOLLHEIM, PUBLISHER

1633 Broadway, New York, NY 10019

DAW Collectors' Book No. 625

First Printing, April 1985

1   2   3   4   5   6   7   8   9

PRINTED IN U.S.A.

CONTENTS

Prologue

In a distant future. . .
Which is very like the past. . . .
When the deserts of the world lie veiled in thick mists, when the precipices of reason have grown steeper and steeper, when the laws of science have been replaced by the teachings of a handful of fanatics. . . .

Science had slipped the hands of scientists. In the power of technological outlaws, it had become a slow-fused bomb, a loose cannon, a slow rot, a cancer. It had spread its ulcers over the whole planet, eating deep into the swollen flesh, its machines and levers biting into the crust with terrible persistence, shattering its bones, corrugating the skin of the Earth itself.

The Great Burning set every volcano on the planet to belching its guts out, even volcanoes long thought extinct, eruptions at every firehole under the sea. The earth's crust was shaken with spasmodic tremors, groaning like a drunkard, heaving like the belly of a woman in labor, birthing monsters by the hundreds, thousands—millions.

Great hurricanes scoured the planet.
Cities sank into the earth.
The earth's axes tilted enough to change the configurations of the continents.
And the face of the earth was changed.
For long, long years.

It took those long, long years, those interminable decades of chaos and red barbarism before it was possible to restore order.
And once that New Order was in place, the world again fell into convulsions.
When the brief but murderous Crystal War erupted, Civilization, already bled white, fell back into barbarism.
A deeper one.
The New Order coiled back on itself like

that legendary serpent that bites its own tail in its sleep, steeped in its own venom and hatred.

Past, present, future—became words without distinction.

I

ARISE, YE WINDS OF DARKNESS

The cold was intense. It clawed at faces, gnawed at the flesh of the hands, seemed bent on gnawing to the bone one's taut muscles, stretched hard as stone. The gonfalons hung on their staffs and the standards stayed motionless, hanging in oily folds, hiding the images of heraldic beasts caged in their velvet prison.

The cold was intense and it grew more so when the night wind rose.

But the warrior in the violet cloak cared little for the assault of the cold. He bent all his attention down the paths of his own mind, a mind glacial as the wind out of the dark, hard as the flints of the devastated roads he followed.

The vast army of the Lords of War was ready to take up the march, ready to begin its hunt.

And that hunt would be long and hard, and bloody.

The horsemen and the infantry of all the fortresses of West and East, of North and South, were gathered under the banner of the Tetrarch of Night, Lord Dmitri Vashar, Knight of the Holy Company, Grand Liegeman of the Great Serpent, Knight of the Right Hand, Guardian of the Tradition and Familiar of the Temple.

"Arise, Wind of Darkness!"

The utterance of Lord Vashar contained as much of command as of prayer, for there was no doubt he truly expected to affect the elements, to bend the sorceries of the shadow to his own energy and determination. And after a moment of excruciating stillness, the nightwind began to sigh.

Crescendo.

Sublime crescendo.

"Come to me, thou wind of night, come to me ye shadows and thou fire, thou poison, thou cold, thou bile and thou blood. . . ."

An electric shudder ran through the army of the Lords of War.

The moment had come to march.

The time had come to wreak vengeance on the men of the Outside.

Nothing could stop them.

A thunder, soft at first, then more and more irresistible, swelled in the ranks of the infantry and the riders, while the gonfalons and the standards strained against the wood and the metal. It became a cry, multiplying, pouring down among the cracks of darkness.

. . . .an explosion of hate.

Dmitri Vashar let his face suffuse with blood; he lifted his eyes toward the sorceries of the moon, toward the bizarre multiplication of the clouds.

The nightwind had answered him.

The wind of hate breathed for him.

For him, Dmitri Vashar, Lord of the Lords of War, Holy Knight, Lieutenant-general of the Fortresses, Grand Liegeman of the Great Serpent, Knight of the Right Hand, Guardian of the Tradition. . . .

For him and his company; for the army he had raised against the rebels who had broken divine law, invaded the possessions of the Elect, and brought fire and massacre into the holy precincts.

The wind of night had revealed its will to the riders and to the ranks of infantry arrayed beneath the oriflammes, the standards, the gonfalons.

While he breathed mightily the strong odors borne on the shadowed winds, he told himself that he had made alliance with the cold, that he had won unto himself the demons of chance, that he had gathered long sundered alliances once more to march under his banner, that he had bridged the ancient rifts which divided the inhabitants of the fortresses.

His hate was strong and hard.

His hate was keen and pure. As crystal. As ice. As the steel of swords.

It was directed entirely toward a young man, a traitor who had offered up his own people to the knives of murderers, and it was directed toward a strange man whose face was the face of a bear.

His hatred was narrow and straight as the blade of a dagger.

His spies had coursed the steppes, the mountains, the plains, the deserts. He had spent entire fortunes and treasures of imagination, he had put to the most hideous tortures those he suspected of hiding from him important information concerning his enemies; he had put entire villages to torch and sword, had had men impaled, had women crucified and infants burned, all to demonstrate by these terrible examples that he would stop at nothing to recover his lost power.

His hatred burned like fire. Burned like the hardest winter ice.

The wind scattered the clouds, and the stars,

colder and more glittering than they had ever been, ranged themselves in their accustomed constellations around the gibbous moon and the faintly glowing point which was Faraway, the fortress in space.

Dmitri Vashar raised his hand and his entire body strained.

The nightwind sang like a drunken demon.

Birds cried out with melancholy in a black sky. A sky as dark and expressionless as the brow of a slave of the Rocky Isles. The wind had sunk away in brief calm and the inkblack clouds hung fixed in the darkness of space, assuming their most chaotic shapes. Behind the barrier which thrust up out of the chill, lead-hued waters, the soiled sails of fishing boats hung limp as dead skin. The rocky barrier, viewed from the side, seemed an artifice, as if it had been reared many years in the past to serve as rampart against the inevitable pirate raids.

Shai and Bearface stood on a rocky outcrop which thrust far out among the waves of this sea. They did not speak, for to men who were accustomed to plains and to forests, to steppes and to mountains, the sea was a fearsome companionship. Although they had been established on this coast for some few months now, they had never grown accustomed to the song

of the waves or the howlings of the storms.
They had made their peace with the indigenes,
obtaining from them a precious aid and quite a
harvest of information. The local fishermen lived
in perpetual terror of the brown-skinned pirates who infested these steep shores so frequently cut with retreats and beaches propitious
to their sudden landings. The most savage of
all were those who had made their lair in a
small desolate archipelago which the autoch-
thones named the Rocky Isles. They had built
there a few forts and even, rumor had it, a
castle of baroque and disturbing architecture,
riddled with traps and snares, pierced with
secret passages and mazed with impossible
burrowings. They practiced, as did all Barbarians of the levant, a slavery that bordered on
the scientific.

Bearface indulged himself in telling a series
of anecdotes, each more awful than the last.
The cruelty of these pirates was proverbial
(perhaps a shade too proverbial even for the
taste of Bearface and Shai) and it seemed far
better to choose death rather than to fall into
their hands. The most fortunate were those
prisoners they kept as slaves: the others perished in atrocious and interminable torture, to
the great amusement of the corsair captains.
As these tortures were meant to impress the
coastal populations, the pirates left very much

in evidence—after each raid—the eloquent remains of these victims of their perverse sense of fantasy.

Bearface shook his head when the chiefs related to him in abundant detail the sufferings of these unhappy victims. When they described what the women were compelled to undergo, they waxed particularly descriptive, and the hetman stopped them frequently with gestures of vexation.

"And then," the storyteller would exclaim, "we scant the truth of it. You had to be there to see it, hetman!"

"I've seen a lot of things here and there, my friends," Bearface declared. "Gloomy and awful things of which you have no idea. Your pirates are dreadful marauders, to be sure, but we will teach them a lesson or two."

"And how are you going to do that, Lord?" the chiefs demanded then, surveying him with incredulity. "We know not what fate has brought you to this place, you and your companions, but we do know that you will not stay here forever. Even if you save us for a little while from these pirates of the Rocky Isles, supposing that you do succeed in that, we will fall again into their hands the moment you turn your backs."

Shai was not pleased that they talked to his comrade in arms after this fashion. "You dotards!

You've become cowardly as aged curs. We've crossed great distances; we've met men and beasts of this world and of another; and *we're* still alive!"

The old chiefs found difficulty in accepting the young man's impertinences, but they made no harsh answer to him, for they feared they might offend these riders who came from the Northern Stars and turn them against their cause.

"We once took a fortress. We held it in our hands."

"A fortress! No one can take a fortress. The walls are too thick, the defenders too well armed."

"We entered by a trick."

"And why," the chiefs asked then sagely, "didn't you stay there, in this fortress which then belonged to you?"

There was a silence. Painful, piercing, almost palpable.

We made a mistake, Bearface thought. And his mindsent message touched Shai. *Aye, I do know it. Our tongues just outstripped our intelligence. . . .*

"We are men of the Outside. Once the secrets of the Doctors were in our hands, we left the fortress to the carrion crows and went back to the plain, the steppes, the forest. What would we have won by shutting ourselves into the high walls of a citadel? We are free men."

Shai shut his eyes, thinking of the flames of the encampment shining under the chill moon and the sea singing them its slow song. He remembered the terrible desolation which attended them in the courts and the platforms, the side streets and the public squares of the ruined citadel. Thousands of ghosts seemed to turn upon him the gaze of their extinguished eyes. Extinguished and yet glowing with the dead fires of hatred. . . . The fortress had been left behind them, left to its hate. A curse weighed upon it.

They had ridden, ridden, ridden without letup, dogged from behind by an inexpressible anxiety, growing, ever-present. It felt as if those eyes had gained wings to fly after them and to track them tirelessly across the plains and the forests, the steppes and the swamps.

During the long days, the long nights, they had had the feeling that the sullen eyes of the Great Serpent had observed the least of their movements, eyes infinitely multiplied, as by some dire and spontaneous generation.

The little band had expected bloody ambush, countless traps, but finally they had reunited themselves with their own people, never encountering any obstacles beyond their own fatigue, their own incertitude.

Bearface's captains found no logical explanation for this behavior. They had suddenly felt themselves suffocating within walls of stone, forbidding towers, shadowed windows which acquired a hundred thousand eyes. They had held counsel at length, in respect to the laws of the plain and the forest, and then they had decided to go their way, taking their captives with them.

They abandoned the fortress of the Great Serpent and the fruits of a shattering victory over the forces of the Enemy.

Gripped in a dull anxiety, which grew and grew.

They had left behind them at Bash a few watchers with instructions to await the return of Bearface and his company. No one ever saw them again. They seemed to have evaporated into the infinite.

Perhaps they had grown weary of waiting, perhaps they had fallen under attack and been captured by some mysterious enemy. Most likely they had been seized by panic, feeling themselves watched by the dead eyes of the fortress, and had purely and simply deserted, preferring a life of banditry to the security in the heart of the horde.

Who could be sure? The enigma, in any case, remained unresolved.

And the fortress of the Great Serpent had

regained its imperturbability, stony serpent, hypocritically asleep in what looked to be an eternal hibernation.

When Bearface, Dorn, Shai, Lsi, Parn, Kjul, and Wran had rejoined the horde, after a second trek in silence and incertitude, the hetman had let his anger fly: for a moment they had held the reins of their destiny in their hands, for a brief twinkle in the eye of eternity they had been able to believe that they had broken the fangs of the Great Serpent. The captains and the other officers had pleaded their case at length. They had felt themselves prisoners of the high walls; they had had a feeling of imminent threat; "as if, at any given moment, invisible warriors were watching our every move."

"What would we have gained by staying shut inside the walls of that old citadel? Did we have to wait for the trap to slam shut on us?"

"What trap?" Bearface had asked then. "What trap are you talking about?"

But the silence, a silence thick as a puddle of congealed blood, had been the only answer to his question.

Rather than further dishearten his captains, the hetman had preferred to throw his men into a new operation.

"We have begun a thing; we have to finish it."

He had launched into a long tale, a tale which glowed with shining imagery, with clever evocations of vastly disparate events, some things perfectly plausible, others legendary or at the very least allegorical.

Shai had admired Bearface's talent. He had never really seen him in the labor of his chiefly duties. He had never appreciated in any proper measure the power which this totemic man wielded over his peers.

The men had hung upon the utterances of their chief, deriving from his tale, his brutal, subtle, colorful, hypnotic narrative, new force, new ideas. No, the world had not stopped living; it beat in the hollow of their hands like a gigantic heart, red and powerful. The world remained full of surprises, of wondrous things to see, and to seize.

They had set out. And on their way they had conquered new lands, built fortified camps, left garrisons to protect their rear.

They had pursued this advance as far as the edge of this sea which they had known only through the tales of caravaneers and the wandering minstrels who sang its mysteries.

After a long, long march, once they had built their new fortified encampment in the shelter of the rocks, there arose among the men, the women, the children, and even among their captives whom they had brought with them on this uncertain enterprise—a stirring of excitement, a great flaring of joy.

And now, on the verge of this distant sea toward which they had ridden for so long, Shai recalled the day of their great setting-forth, when, subject to the words of Bearface, the riders had let their enthusiasm break forth: the hetman was going to lead them from victory to victory, to the very end of the earth.

Alas, he had the impression, seeing again those men galloping down the great avenue of the camp, remembering the glittering of the axes and the lances, the knives and the sabers brandished in the sunlight—aye, he had the impression, and he could not shake it off, that Bearface's army had come to dead stop at the end of the world.

To build a town. . . .

To build it and ring it round with solid walls.

But the nomads hesitated. To shut themselves in, they said, inside stone ramparts, was it not to enter decline, to rust away, to lose what created their strength: their mobility?

"We came here to build a town. A town which will be powerful enough to protect us against our enemies. We have proved that the gods were false gods. Don't let the Serpent recover his strength and his venom. Be reasonable with yourself, hetman!"

The black birds still screamed in the black sky.

The dark clouds multiplied in the deceptive light. Black gut festooned with menacing growths of fungus. A stormy aggregation of quicksilver and soot. The melancholy of the landscape became unbearable.

"I had a strange dream," said the hetman, "a drunken shaman's dream. There was a red sun in the sky, a sun which was like a giant eye. An immense lid covered it, which winked slowly, with a sort of malice. A great tear fell on the earth, a red tear, hot and burning. It looked like lava, or blood. And this red, hot, burning tear—covered the earth, slowly, wearing a path toward me. I was standing on a little mound of dry grass and I couldn't move, couldn't make a move to run. Slowly the giant tear rolled toward me, while in the burning sky the strange eye gathered another droplet.

"Slowly the bloody flood kept coming, burning the dry grass in its passage, coming closer and closer to me, in spite of obstacles it covered or flowed round—it was as if it *knew* what it had to do. Then there was a rumbling, a long sound like voices, and I saw a band of black riders come down from the sky and ride straight toward me, as if the bloody tear had opened the way for them. A burning pain reached my feet, a grip along my legs; the black riders were brandishing weapons that glittered in the night. I woke drenched in sweat and for a long while after that dream stayed with me and I was unable to put any order in my thoughts. I have had more frightening dreams in my life, and I don't understand why that one so got its claws into me, imbedded itself so strongly in my memory. Can you explain it to me?"

Shai smiled. But it was a smile without mockery in it, a smile vaguely troubled. He chose a pleasantry in the way of an answer. "Even shamans sometimes grow afraid of their dreams. And even hetmen grow old."

"Maybe you're right," said Bearface. "I have gotten old. You've made me read too many books; you've made me put my hands on too many strange things I don't understand much about. Beyond a doubt, I have too many ambitions for my people, too many dreams without a tomorrow. . . ."

The black birds had finally flown away. They seemed to have been breathed out by a thick ragged cloud in the bosom of which poured a vast funnel of shadows. Shai would have wished the stars to come back, to lighten this gloomy strand with their pale shining, to lessen the sorrow of this night.

"You were never as strong as you are at this moment," the young man said, a little numbly.

"It's the color of this night that gives you the vapors."

"Shai, my son, I don't know what you mean by vapors, but maybe you're right: plainsmen are very susceptible to atmospheres. I've seen men break down and cry for no other cause than the melancholy of an autumn night or because the wind whispered in dry grass in a certain way. And it is true ... There's something about this night."

The young man shivered, but he spoke in a kind of bravado. "What do you think it's saying, this night?"

Bearface did not answer. His thoughts wandered elsewhere, in an ocean of pitch where the starswarm perished by drowning.

Suddenly he said, following the logic of his thoughts: "The wind, maybe ... it can't make up its mind to blow, to chase this dark away."

Shai felt ill at ease now. He regretted letting himself be drawn onto this sinister shore far from the fortified camp, hidden in the arc of this rocky circle, at the foot of the first ramparts of these ocher mountains. He ought to have been sleeping next to Lsi, his comrade of days both good and bad. They would have talked softly together in this suffocating darkness. Aye, they would have talked for a long time before letting themselves be carried into sleep—or love. Thinking of the young woman he felt a knot of warmth gather in his groin. He lost the thread of the conversation.

Slowly they walked along the shore. The surf churned the black pebbles while the frenetic crabs fled clattering their gigantic claws. The silence of the sea weighed on them—a crushing weight—and suddenly, as if at a signal, the wind rose.

The nightwind, with its feathery touches and its murmurings, its heavy laments and its furious cries, its threats and its unbridled tempers. It wrapped them both in its cloak of cold and vapors, its moisture and its salt.

The clouds took flight, approached rapidly from another quarter of space, tearing away large portions of the storm-soiled sky, marked with the pustule of the ruddy moon, sundering the stars into surreal configurations. In this cosmic absurdity he searched for the second of Earth's moons, Faraway, the high-orbital station in its gloomy mysteries; Faraway, the Great Dragon of the Sky. Burning recollections crossed his memory: the grinning face of Dr. Pfeil, the master of the swamps, and yet more enigmatic, the face of Syria, whose perfumed lies had led him along fiery corridors, through the labyrinths of Earth's antiquity.

He misstepped on a rocky rise and gave a startled cry. His dreams fled, vanished into the gulf of stars. The night wind snarled now like an angry cat. A blue light shimmered in the heavens. A light which seemed to debate which path to follow. Fffft. It went out like a soap-bubble, bursting without warning.

This strange luminous phenomenon, which was perhaps nothing but an insignificant meteor, appeared to him as evil augury.

We are here to build a town, Shai said to himself. *We have come to the edge of this sea to raise solid walls and fortify ourselves against our enemies, against those who will someday come against us to exact vengeance for the past. And now, as if their former victories have terrified them, in facing a destiny too great for them, the captains hesitate, and the hetman himself speaks in riddles, hides himself behind symbols, images, and entire damned mythology. Yes, damned—eventually. We came here to build a town.*

"It's true," Shai said aloud, "we came here to build a town. After your men found the citadel too oppressive for their superstitious souls."

"I know we traveled all this way, we fought battles without number, to raise walls and build a new civilization; but we are all outdoorsmen, we, and we suffer from a strange malady."

—From claustrophobia, my friend. From claustrophobia. That's what my books call this sickness.

—You can call the sickness whatever name

you like. We're in the habit of doing things slowly, soberly, after we've gotten together. You expect us to change that in a few seasons?

—Your thoughts have a strange color today, Bearface, and I have the impression that you hardly trust yourself. And then, admit it, it isn't uncommon for you to on impulse, for you to break everything under the hooves of your horses—

—Our horses often make our decisions! the hetman cried. "Let's leave this child's game, Shai. Let's stop playing mind-games."

They walked in silence along the shore.

The birds glided over the surface of the spray-crested waves, heavy liquid masses dashing against the rocky barrier. Sometimes the birds' malefic cries rose above the clash of the waves. They hurled thankless voices against the wind, which broke on the salt, ragged crests of the hurricane which raised itself between sea and sky like a mix of rippled fire.

Bearface and Shai did not delay: in a moment the storm would break in earnest, cover the beach with its creeping tentacles, gouge viciously at the rocky escarpments, roar and low like a stubborn beast that knows its battle will never cease, that it has neither rhyme nor reason, but which raves and hurls all its might into the struggle.

"We will build this town," said the hetman. "I make my oath on it."

Lsi waked with a start.

She was drenched with sweat. Her nightgown clung to her sticky flesh and brief but powerful waves of nausea came in spasms, bending her double.

What an awful dream!

She walked on the beach. The shingle was quite peaceful in the misty morning. One could scarcely see the sea, so thick the fog was. She routed before her entire colonies of largish crabs. She could have gathered them for food, for their flesh was edible, even delicate. But she was content to walk along the beach, lost in morose thoughts (truly, morose?)—and the veil of mist had given way as if a cruel and pitiless hand had seized it in iron fingers—a rider had emerged from the sea, all clothed in black, his eyes aflame. His white hair seemed to have been encrusted in salt; with that kind of stiffness and pallor. It was quite likely it should not lie down properly and if—the stranger clutched the reins in a hand the veins of which swelled repulsively and in the other hand, gloved in black, he brandished a strange weapon.

"What are you looking for here?" he asked in a thunderous voice. And she did not know what to tell him. "You don't know that death lives in

these regions, like. . . ." (His voice lost itself in the fog as he drove his horse toward her.)

"Please," she cried, "I don't know who you are, but don't talk to me like that!"

Indistinct, indescrible shapes (but suspect and menacing all the same) moved behind the curtain of mist that suddenly sealed itself behind the dark rider's back. "You don't guess what comes from the sea?" asked the centaur of pitch and salt.

Something, as if to confirm the threats of the apparition, encircled the milky wall like a whiplash, a sort of long spiny whip. And Lsi fell to her knees on the sand, her heart clutched by a fear more devastating than that which she had felt when she was the prisoner of Leaf, and—

"Remember my words!"

The spiny thing which had cut the fog flung itself around her body and a venomed burning bit her to the bone—

What a dreadful dream!

When Shai entered the hut, she flung herself into his arms.

She told him her nightmare with much chattering of teeth and he did not know what to do but to say over and over to her the words he hoped would calm her.

"It's nothing," he said, forcing a calm upon himself, "it's nothing at all. It's just the nightwind. It blows over one's nerves when one sleeps and suggests frightful dreams. . . . Everything's all right now, everything's all right."

He rambled. And he knew it. Something was coming. Something was coming in the night. Something frightful and inexorable.

"It's only the nightwind. You hope it will come to drive the clouds and make the stars come back, but sometimes—often—it only brings monsters. You have to try to sleep. Come."

He gently caressed her hair, searched the salt planes of her cheeks with his lips, but she suddenly clung to him with a sort of uncontrollable madness, which was not usual in her, pouring poignant obscenities into his ear. *Do it now,* she begged him, *yes, do it to me now, I can't wait any longer, come on—*

But Shai had no heart for it. He would have rather rested unmoving at Lsi's side. To help her conquer her pain by his mere presence.

"Where were you all this time? Awful—it was awful. Come, oh, come, make love to me."

Lsi's hands were claws on his neck, on his back, and he shivered. For a brief instant he thought he saw a light shine in the young woman's eyes like the eyes of a maddened beast—or like the eyes of the lycanthropes with which the men of the plains and forest people their cruel legends.

"Lsi!"

"Yes, yes, yes, I *am* Lsi! What do you *expect* me to be? I need you, I need your warmth in me—"

She began to unbuckle Shai's belt.

He expected her hands to be burning hot.

But they were like claws of ice.

Impatient, brutal.

The nightwind groaned like an animal wounded to the death.

In its madness it sank its teeth into human flesh.

Dmitri Vashar's jaws stayed clenched, as if bolted shut. Painful cramps afflicted his jaw muscles. The road was still long to the citadel of Orghedda, but he had decided they would march to the foot of the Jermyn hills, and the murmurs of his officers were nothing but importunate gnats: he had dismissed them with a disdainful wave of his hand.

My hate, he said to himself, as if he recited a prayer, *my hate is hot as fire—burning as the ice of deepest winter. My hate is strong and hard. My hate is sharp and pure. As crystal. As ice.—As the steel of a sword.*

In a few days they would reach the citadel of Orghedda, the proudest, most impenetrable of the fortresses of the Great Serpent. They would assemble there in the last complete council of war.

There would be thousands gathered under the banner of the Great Serpent. The battle against the unbelievers would be war without mercy.

It would not end until all the rebels had been bowed before the law. When the Outsiders had seen their own blood flow, when they had understood the vanity of their efforts, when. . . .

The hands of the guardian of the tradition resembled the hands of a stone statue: they seemed frozen to the reins.

The seasons had passed like clouds chased by an impetuous wind, but the passage of time had changed nothing of the order of things. The fortress of Bash had been taken by forfeit. It had bled from four veins, spread its essence into the earth, was no more than a haunted memory.

He had come back to contemplate it, this stone carcass in a vacant land: all that remained of a proud citadel. Not the grandest nor the strongest, but the most pregnant with mystery, magic, knowledge. *The Citadel of the Great Serpent.*

Rage had churned in his entrails.

A rage which must find its outlet quickly: with his riders he had crossed the no man's land, penetrated into the deserted temple enclosure. The shoes of the horses thundered in this sepulchral void, drew from the pavings of the Court of Arms only hollow echoes.

Later they had discovered in the tortuous windings of the alleyways a few enemy partisans dead drunk. They had taken them without striking a blow, had tortured them to get from them information about Shai and the rebel chief, but whether they were inured to pain, or they were ignorant of the actions of their masters, the nomads died without betraying them, dismembered, castrated, reduced to merest shreds.

There had been much of that.

Dmitri Vashar began to lost all concept of time.

He turned toward the somber silhouette which rode at his side, silent shadow, patient and discreet. Under the hood, red eyes gleamed, white gloved hands, bizarrely deformed, held the reins of a dark horse.

"There," said Dmitri Vashar, "lie the corpses of our laws, there rots the spoilage of the tradition. You understand me, don't you, Shag? . . . Yes, I know you do. The hate and the rage that live in me, you are perhaps the only one who can understand the extent of them, who can comprehend how far they reach." Dmitri Vashar gave a dark laugh, a laugh in which there was not the least spark of joy. "In this citadel, within these walls which ought to have protected the knowledge of the ancients, which ought to. . . ."

His voice lost itself in the wind, and the somber, funereal shadow in the monk's hood gave a kind of pathetic laugh, as if it had tried to echo the laugh of the Tetrarch of Night.

Then a croaking voice came from amongst those shadows. "Time," it said, "master, it belongs to you. Confusion on our enemies."

Parenthesis III

THE GRAY DAWNS OF FARAWAY

(They consumed themselves and died. They were mechanisms that had grown too old.) They had become obsolete; images inverted in a mirror, grotesque personages, already evanescent, in a shadow-play to which no audience had come in a very, very long time.

They lived on a strange world which went on existing around them and which would certainly be there when they all were gone. An artificial world created aboard a gigantic orbiting station named Faraway, or named, again, Skydragon, a magnificent enclosure open at its every bay to the solar winds that swept the interplanetary void. Faraway, tenth planet in the solar system, pride of the human race, giant space village, peopled with sad ghosts.

The gray morning of Faraway had long forgotten the vast sunshine of conquest, though the hydroponic gardens would still and for generations to come, be sufficient to provision numerous starfaring vessels.

On a bridge which spanned in its single arch a limpid pond, in the very bosom of a park which was twin to some Japanese garden, a man and a woman stood in converse, pitched low as if that conversation could have been disturbed by chance strollers. This occurred during one of those gray dawns which were usual on Faraway, brusque shifts of light, without importance or seriousness but productive of bizarre attacks of anxiety. For these sudden flashes of intense illumination—would they not afford these creatures who lived scattered through a world suspended between Earth and Moon, the clearest, the most exquisite awareness of their own fragility?

On this bridge, apart from the principal aggregation that was Skydragon, this man and this woman spoke softly. Above their heads, through the great window that opened upon the powdery outside night, came burning spindles of gray light.

"We consume ourselves and die," the young woman said. But she was not really young any longer. She was beautiful, but ageless. "Yes, we consume ourselves and we die . . . and it's not fair! The machines go on working, never reproducing, and they repair themselves forever. According to codified, coded instructions imprinted in their memory cells. You and I, my love, we're less than the machines."

The man shook his head. "No one," he said, with a sort of rage that boiled and bubbled at the depth of his voice, "no one can be *less* than a machine. Never say that."

She lifted her skirt over milk-white thighs. "Take this off," she said, "take me here, right now. The blood rushes to my head, I feel hot, like fever. Don't think, don't say anything. Impregnate me, here, standing, now, try to come off in me, try—maybe, O god, god, god, it'll work this time!"

The man jerked his companion's slip away and penetrated her standing, furiously, teeth clenched. Working at her, thrusting at her, he could not stop crying. "O Lord, Lord, remake my insides, make me, make us fertile!"

II
THE OLD MAN OF THE CLIFF

The gray-eyed chief shook his head slowly. "You must consult the shaman," he said in a heavy voice. "Such dreams are predictors of disease and death, surely of catastrophes."

Shai tried to catch the old man's glance, but the old man pointedly turned his head, stirring the dying embers with the end of his stick. The fire at his feet was no more than a heap of wood and blackened seaweed.

"You know, you do know something, but you aren't willing to tell me. I do adjure you, chief, tell me what this dream means."

"I'm not a shaman, I'm not privy to the secrets of the gods. Your wife had a bad dream, a

very bad dream. What can I tell you about it?
So. Go see the shaman!"

It was always the way with the dwellers on
the coast. Conversations ended abruptly, turning back upon themselves.

These old chiefs were prudent: as a result of
being so often beaten down and victimized they
had chosen a mode of elocution which kept
their verbal equilibrium as deftly as a fortune-
teller. When they felt themselves pushed to
their last retreat, they invariably cried: "Go
see the shaman!"—but when one did go to the
sorcerer, the matter went from bad to worse.
For the shamans were past masters of the art
of finding their direction out by indirections:
The habitude of fear had made them with-
drawn and secretive, ambiguous of interpreta-
tion, difficult to love.

"You ought to consult the shaman," the chief
repeated doggedly.

Shai shrugged and shivered in the gray winter light which penetrated to their sitting-place
beneath the little windows of the hut. He hated
the seacoast winter: it took on a sullen charac-
ter predisposed to storms and to pirate raids.
The cold, if it was less bitter than the cold of
the interior of the continent, in the hinterland
where people perished of starvation and despair,
showed itself here more insidious, more piercing.
It slipped under the skin like an blade of ice.

"Maybe if you aren't willing to talk—"

The chief threw him a disquieted glance, hiding like a sick cat within the depth of his hiding-hole. "What?" His voice, stripped of its pretenses, had the inflections of sudden disquietude. *"What?"*

"—we won't defend you, we won't defend you *any longer* against the corsairs' piratical operations—"

The chief hawked and spat into the depths of the foyer.

"You can't do that."

"I have no choice, chief. I'm forced to take measures to force you to come out of your shell. What would you do in my place?"

Shai felt the anger in the chief's soul, the more burning because fueled with the accumulated impotence of decades.

If he dared, he would break his chief's baton over my skull. He's old and full of experience and I, what am I in his eyes, but a young sot, a popinjay whose cockiness is intolerable to him, an insult more hurtful than spitting in his face.

"Chief, do understand me. I respect you for your wisdom and your knowledge, but I need to know this."

"I thought you were a boy from the fortresses. I thought you had read more books than the sky has stars. You ought to know what a simple dream means, a nightmare—"

"I told you: those who live in the citadels believe they own the truth. They think that the world belongs to them, even if they never go outside their four walls except to track a man down and renew their blood. Their certitudes made them sterile long before their victory could ever have become a reality."

"Listen to me. We *here*, we know certain things about the past, about the terrible events which occurred in this country and in others, more distant from us." He coughed, like an experienced orator, and spat sententiously into the dying coals. "Yes, that's good, sit down there . . . near me. I could be your father twice over and I have an affection for you. Yes, that's right, chew a little of this herb, it will give you a pleasant sensation, it will make everything comfortable in your stomach. We all, in this village, and in the other villages which line this coast, we all have sworn an oath."

Shai who, for courtesy's sake, chewed distractedly at the blue weed, looked up to hear from the chief's own lips the revelations which had become important to him.

"We all have taken oath to the . . . the Old Man of the Cliff. We have all sworn to him on the heads of our first-born that we will keep to ourselves both his existence and the place where he hides. The Old Man of the Cliff, at the time when he was still full of vigor, fought at our side against the pirates. He taught us what he himself used to call his tricks. But one day he left us. He had become too old. Too frail. As he left he lifted up his hands and gave us, us the chiefs, the shamans, his blessing. Then he swore that he would pray for us, each and every day, that things would fall back into order. Before he turned his horse toward the cliffs, he had exacted the promise of which I spoke a moment ago and which I have just now broken. A curse upon me!"

Go on talking, old chief, go on talking, your promise doesn't help you at all any longer.

"Go on."

"Oh, you are impatient. You are all bubbling with your youth. Good, I'm going to satisfy that curiosity that must burn your stomach like envy. I can't help but think that your friend in her dream—she's seen the old man of the cliff in person . . . if I dare say—"

"She never saw him in the flesh and no one, things being as things are, ever spoke to her about him. How do you explain that phenomenon? Must I believe in prophecies which come to us from dreams?"

"I don't know enough to tell you. I'm not a shaman. It must be the fourth time I've told you this. All I can tell you is this, that the description Lsi made of the rider with the white hair is very like the appearance of our old friend. Maybe he's immortal."

"No one is. Superstition."

"Really? You're like some young animal that pisses on everything it doesn't understand. You'll die young if you spurn certain advice. . . ."

"I don't spurn it. If I did would I be here in your house, trying to drag it out your nose? But I interpret things differently. I'd like to know where the old man of the cliff used to live."

The old chief grinned and spat again. "In the cliff, of course."

"Hah. You got me. I act like a young imbecile, but the cliff is vast, a veritable labyrinth. Be a little more precise."

"I love thee well, lad. Sometimes you can be sharp as a sword, devious as an old shaman. That's well. You'll know it all. But I beg you, try to have some care for my honor. I wouldn't want to go about in the eyes of all the world as an oathbreaker. Don't make me lose face, young man."

The chief advanced the conversation in the sidelong manner of a crab, but Shai knew that his point was won. In a few moments, just the time it took for an ambuscade of his honor, the old chief had told him everything. He wondered with a little touch of vexation why he ever attached so much importance to Lsi's dream.

The blue weed had enveloped him now. He was adrift in a lake of gauzy resistance. "I take all the responsibility. You have my word."

The chief gave a wily chuckle. But then he spoke without pause, as if he wished to unburden himself of the subject as rapidly as possible. While he told the tale of the old man of the cliff he kept his eyes lowered, doubtless conscious that he was not acting within the law of his tribe. When he had finished his tale he nudged Shai with his baton. "Now that you know it all, go, quick, get out of here."

Shai and Dorn followed a steep path which wandered along the cliffs. From the place where they were now, they began to ascend among rocks of tormented aspect, that thrust up like sabers and daggers, monstrous teeth rising out of the mist. The dwarf maintained a *sotto voce* soliloquy, cursing the ill fortune which obliged him to follow the young madman in his tomorrowless enterprises.

"Your doddering chief really took you for a fool in this one, lad. You're going to break your neck and I can't help you. I'll have to make up some likely story for the hetman when you end up broken on the rocks." The gnome ground his teeth in anger. A rock had just slipped under his foot, and he narrowly escaped losing his balance.

Shai shrugged his shoulders. "Do pay attention, Dorn, you know anger goeth before a fall—"

"Young fool!" Then he suddenly recovered his composure and began to laugh. "You still aren't going to convince me any rider could have passed this road without us finding him in small pieces, a hundred meters down. And the road is getting narrower."

Shai wondered if the dwarf did not have the right idea: it could well be that the chief, desirous of maintaining the secret, had sent him on a wild goose chase. A chase from which he had almost no chance of returning alive.

A flood of adrenalin rushed into his bloodstream as he found himself suddenly adangle between sea and sky, clinging by both hands to a frail out-thrust of rock. An iron fist closed about his heart, while another hand of prodigious strength seized upon his heels and drew him toward the chasm, toward the thundering floods which churned below him. He was going to die, he was going to die a fool's death.

On an impulse. Because of a whim of curiosity which was at best ill-counseled and which someone, perhaps advisedly, had breathed into his ear . . .

"I'm going to die!"

"You're not going to die, fool! You're going to open your eyes and look straight in front of you. The height's put bugs in your brain. Don't look down, if you don't want to fall! A damn long drop, poor idiot!"

When I get back, Shai told himself, *I'm going to have a word with the chief with the gray eyes. I'm going to ask him some more questions. Yes, but will I ever get back? Don't look down, above all don't look down. . . .*

Rounding a corner of the rock, the path grew suddenly wider, and they could proceed at their ease, without having to flatten themselves against the rock wall.

But with the best will in the world and all the skill an experienced horseman could muster, no one could ever have been fool enough to force a horse along this rocky trail. Without a doubt the rider from the seacliff was nothing but a myth, and it might even have happened that in the course of some conversation with the folk of the coast, Lsi had gotten wind of a forbidden legend, babbled in bits and pieces in the smoke of the blue weed. The path swerved abruptly between two rocky spires, a blue skewed square opening in the rock, under the crystalline blue sky, void of all accumulation of cloud. They entered with a sort of respectful slowness, for they had the impression that this was a forbidden domain. Past the gateway of this strange tabernacle, they found themselves in a short rocky corridor which thrust straight into the summit of the cliff. A hidden place which no one could have guessed as he came from the sea and which, year in year out, must have escaped all the pirates' investigations. A luminous incline—a fiery brazen serpent, coiled along the rock, lighting the varied stones of the passage with subtle colorations: they shut their eyes against the assaults of this jeweled barrage. Then when they stopped at a loud rattle of stone, a voice spoke, distinctly, separating one word from the other.

"I don't know who you are, but if you come another step closer, I'll kill you." The words rolled along the rocky corridor, echoing through the blue silences in which even the thunder of the surf was drowned. "Let me see your faces. If you have weapons, throw them down!"

"Don't do it," Dorn mutered in a voice so low it came out no more than a throaty murmur. *"He'll kill us anyway!"*

"I said, throw down your weapons! You won't be mad enough to walk around up here without weapons!"

In order not to encumber themselves on the cliffside road, Shai and Dorn had brought nothing but daggers passed through their heavy leather belts.

The blasters, slung behind them, were for

the moment unusable. In the time it would take to loose them from their straps their still-invisible adversary would lay them both stiff on the ground. They dropped their daggers on the ground and stood motionless, their eyes narrowed.

"You're trying to put one over on me! The lasers! Take them off and put them at your feet. God! I wonder where primitives like you could have gotten such treasures. . . . Good, now you can move forward. Ah! Not so fast. Slowly. One step after the other, and put your hands on your heads."

Persuaded that he risked no further unpleasant surprise, the mysterious assailant showed himself in full light. There could be no doubt: this was the man they called The Old Man of the Cliff; and Lsi had described him precisely. But this time he wore on his white hair a wide-brimmed hat of an indefinite hue. At his flank he balanced a weapon twice as long as one of Dorn's arms. A weapon which only remotely resembled a blaster.

"What do you mean coming here?" the old man asked.

"I came to see you, to talk with you . . . if you're willing to listen."

"And how did you learn of my existence? And who has shown you the way to my refuge? It was a secret most closely kept."

Shai hesitated to answer. Momentarily he examined the tall figure clad in mismatched garments, crowned with that strange headgear, hands clenched upon what was surely an ancient weapon, to judge by its polish and its bizarre shape, old but very certainly still very dangerous. If he spoke too quickly he risked fouling things up for once and all.

It was Dorn who answered—with a chuckle and a gibe. "Only fools imagine that their secrets remain forever inviolate. Especially considering everyone thinks you dead."

The barrel of the weapon threatened them with greater precision. "Go on like that. I'm going to put a bullet in your head for your impertinence."

Dorn shrugged. "You're half dead already," he retorted. "Kill us and you *will* be dead. Even up here in the cliffs you must have gotten wind of our coming. Our whole horde is camped not far from here. With weapons and baggage. Hundreds of riders, with their women, their children, their—"

A detonation shook the rocks round about. The echo of it had a particularly expressive whine.

"The next time will be it," said the old man of the cliff. "Take that for the truth."

*　　*　　*

The old man of the cliff lived in an extravagant structure. A sort of shelter made of blocks of stone and pieces of tent fabric. With bits and pieces of a thick door of massive wood (where could he have gotten such a construction, with its carvings shredded with weathering?) whose slit openings let him defend himself effectively against chance improbable intrusions into his rocky domain.

In the interior and in spite of an oppressive gloom, Shai discovered a few implements of suspicious modernity. Instruments the use or usefulness of which he but scarcely understood, but which undoubtedly could not come from a village of fishermen, from a burg of the hinterland or from some deserted fortress.

"Why do you look at me like that?" asked the old man. His eyes blazed with an uncommon fire, vaguely feverish.

"In my books—" Shai began.

"You read books and go about armed with a laser. Where do you come from?"

Shai did not answer. A sarabande of images danced in his head, fleeting memories. . . . He recalled the isle in the swamps, the rotunda which birthed wonders and prodigies; he visited again the oneiric menagerie of Dr. Pfeil.

"Sit down, both of you. And stay quiet. On that condition, you can talk." His gestures belied his words, for he went to sit down at a quite respectable distance, his weapon balanced across his knees.

"You aren't from here," the young man said. "I have just understood that. You come from up there. From the orbiting station."

"You sure about that?" There was irony in the old man's voice, but there was also bitterness.

"Sure as I can be. But I don't understand. Your friends became incapable of breathing Earth's air. They were dying of it, eventually. And. . . ."

"Shit, lad." The weapon was again trained on Shai and his companion. "Where did you learn that? Not in your book, that I do know. It would of course be better for me to liquidate you forthwith."

"Please! Don't point with that weapon. I met your friends on an island, very far from this place, in the middle of a swamp called the Locus Draconis. They were living under the orders of a man they called Dr. Denner Pfeil. A—"

"I'm dreaming. Lad, tell me that I'm dreaming. You did really just speak of Dr. Pfeil. That old windbag is still alive! God!" The old man's hands trembled so much that Shai thought he was going to pull the trigger by accident. "Perhaps you believed what they told you there, on that damned island, where they lived in fear, the way they lived in fear on their artificial planet, my young friend, but those people, my old compatriots of space, they don't know how to live any longer. They're only capable of surviving. And yet— It's all in their head. I'm the living proof. I'm here in front of you, Shai, and I don't wear a helmet or a protective suit. I had the courage to leave that island in space, and after that the island of the dragon. And I traveled among the men of Earth. Sometimes, alas, I lost my way in very bitter reflections. I had become a sort of living fossil, a memory made of flesh and bone. I've fought a great many battles, and I still remember terrible days, days red as blood, black as night. I've killed dozens of men. First with a laser pistol I took with me in my flight, then, later, with less modern weapons I found in the ruins. I tried to create a state down there, in a hundred places. But I was ashamed of my vile tendencies and I came here, followed by the hatred of this Dr. Denner Pfeil . . . No, in spite of appearances, I am not nearly as old as he, but I've lived hard and I don't use the modern techniques of remaking the face. But I talk, I talk, I confound your soul—"

Shai discovered by now that the old man of the cliff had a tendency to monologue. Words flowed from his mouth like water from a leaky spigot. Nervously he shifted his legs, which had gotten an antlike prickle. Now he regretted his adventure with Dorn, for it had manifestly brought him nothing of tangible benefit. The man of the cliff, extraterrestrial or not, was nothing but a senile old man, on the downward side of his decrepitude.

"The men of the coast said you left them riding a horse, and that—"

"On a horse, yes, I did. But I interrupted you again."

"I was wondering how you could have gotten to this hiding place with a horse. It's unthinkable that—"

"I didn't come on this road. No, to you I shall tell the truth: I killed my horse . . . and I ate him. At least half of him."

Shai flinched. The old man dismayed him. He babbled anything.

"You ate your horse."

"No, I'm still lying to you. I killed him, but I buried him in the sand, and I wept. What would you expect me to do with a horse in these cliffs? Anyhow, my horse had injured himself running on the shingles." Tears came to the old man's eyes and rolled down his cheeks, freely, without his attempting to hold them back. "I would have chosen to die myself rather than to eat my horse."

Then he burst out laughing. "A horseman who eats his horse—that's unthinkable!" He laughed the louder. "Can a man eat his own flesh?" He howled. "Tell me! Can any man worthy of the name eat what lies between his legs?"

Dorn broke in with a wheeze. "All right. You're an old fool and you're driving us crazy with your ranting!"

"There are other fools. Pfeil's lot, they're the madmen. Me, I know what I'm doing. And especially I know who and where my enemies are."

Dorn regretted letting his weapons be taken from him. The interview was taking a decidedly upsetting turn.

"I would still be wiser to kill you out of hand. I never asked you to come here." He cleared his throat and declared without preamble: "Fool! Listen to me! The people up there, the people in the space station claim they're sterile. But I, I've lived with many women and sired sons and daughters. Vigorous and viable. What do you say to that?"

Shai shook his head. "I wouldn't want things to get off on the wrong foot between us. I know that you're right, in fact I came to ask you for your advice about a dream."

"A dream! Why on earth would you do that? Have I the look of a village soothsayer, lad? You expect me to read the stars, the tarot, the dreams, the patterns of the sand, when the sea—"

"My wife Lsi had a dream where you appeared to her on horseback. You warned her of some great danger. I expected that you would have found some explanation here in your retreat."

"And who told you I haven't?"

Dorn chuckled. "Old dodderer, you expect us to believe that you're a great savant who's discovered the key to dreams?"

Now with the brutal vitality of the snake, the old man seized the stock of his weapon. Before either of them could react he held Dorn and Shai in his sights.

"You want me to ventilate you with this thing, you poor sods, you great clowns, want me to make you lose your taste for insults?"

"Fire then, you old liar, *fire!*"

Shai felt his blood turn to ice. "Dorn, I beg you! We came here with peaceful intent."

"The road to hell and death is paved with good intentions!" Dorn kept on chuckling, but to himself, almost in silence. He still put on a vague show of arrogance, but Shai knew that he had lost. He had been prepared for a fight to the death and in spite of that, the truly ophidian swiftness with which the old man had seized up his weapon had paralysed him. That was at least the impression he gave: only his eyes remained lively, all agleam with an indomitable hatred.

"Now that you're calm, dear friends, I'm going to tell you ... Once upon a time, long before the events which transformed the face of the world, in an age which now lives only on the other side of memory, there was a brave old man, a kind of sorcerer, who was called the old man of the mountain. He lived surrounded by a band of cutthroats whom he caused to eat a sort of concoction the composition of which remains secret to this day. This concoction, legend tells us, made the warriors courageous and invincible. In any event, they gave the impression that they were, and they did at once anything the old brigand told them to do. Perhaps I might have dreamed of being one day like that old man. From my clifftop I might have reigned over a whole nation of submissive slaves. With what I know of the manipulation of the brain and the conscience, with what I retain of Dr. Denner Pfeil's teachings, I would certainly have been able to put together a fine band of assssins."

"And why didn't you impose your power on the men of the Coast?"

"Lassitude. To become the crownless king of a brutish nation—that is not an ambition worthy of a man who has known the glories and the terrors of interplanetary space."

Suddenly, even as the old man spoke, plunging himself yet deeper into his rambling monologue, a great shadow passed before the open window: a bloody-beaked bird dived into the room, as if it were hurled into the livid light by some invisible force. It gave a long malefic croak, darting its dark metallic beak.

Dorn stood up, forgetting the barrel of the rifle was still trained upon them. The apparition of the bird had provoked in him a sensation of panic fear and he reacted without even having had the time to think clearly, to analyze the situation. A little dagger which he had drawn from his boot suddenly shone in his grip: *"No!"* cried the old man. *"It's tame!"* And he pulled the trigger of his weapon. The projectile whined very near Dorn's ear, went off into the shadows. A split second later Shai had done nothing, not even gesture toward either one of the protagonists of the drama, but the dagger was buried up to the hilt in the throat of the old man of the cliff.

The bird screamed. (Aye, one could not describe the strange and lugubrious cry it gave as it saw its master stagger. *It screamed!* As if it was about to hurl invective at him who had mortally wounded the old man.) Then it hurled itself upon Dorn, claws and beak, eyes redder than droplets of lava. It beat at his breast, attacked his head and eyes. The small man had difficulty in defending himself: the bird was thickly feathered and anger doubled its strength.

Swiftly Shai gathered up the gun. Restraining the tremor of his hands, holding his breath, he sighted upon the moving target, uncertain where the bird's darting head might be. The detonation deafened him momentarily and he staggered with the effect of the recoil. The stock had, maliciously, bruised his right cheek.

Luck had been with him. For, raising a strident lament, the bird beat its wings, loosed its grip and plummeted to the ground. It took only a few seconds to die.

Shai bent over the old man. His lips moved slowly, and it was clear that he was trying to say something before expiring. Shai, ignoring the blood which flowed from the grimacing lips, put his ear to the dying man's mouth ... and heard a strange thing.

"Ah. I've stopped believing that I'm immortal."

III
THE PIRATES

They descended somberly toward the abodes of the inhabitants of the coast. They both knew—and Dorn seemed, since the murder of the old man, to have lost a great deal of his arrogance—that they had just disturbed an established order of things; that they had been rendered culpable of a crime for which they must pay dear, very dear, with new privations and new passages in shadow. But they felt confusedly that they now owed a debt to some mysterious power.

On that return journey, they recovered their blasters and their daggers but they looked on these weapons with revulsion—as if these things could suddenly turn upon them.

They did not speak.

Or they hardly spoke. Except to warn each other of dangers in the path.

Shai cursed the chief, cursed the shaman, these pitiable puppets who had spread for them a trap the consequences of which passed the limits of their feeble understandings. Manifestly they had come away guilty.

"Your chief," said the dwarf, when they were no more than a few steps from the fisherman's huts, "I shall strangle with the cords of my whip. You would do well to do the same with the shaman."

Shai said nothing. He continued to see the blood on the lips of the old man of the cliff and to hear him speak—*Ah. I have stopped believing that I'm immortal.* Such derision in the face of death seemed worst of all. An inadmissable attitude? Grotesquerie? Lack of humanity?

Shai's hands trembled.

He dreaded coming face to face with Lsi, with Bearface. *What shall I tell them then? What shall I tell them now?*

The moon above the sea was gray, clay-colored, traced with broken, unaccustomed lines. The shining mote which was Faraway had disappeared. Lies. Illusions.

They walked at last upon the shingle. The descent had been terrible but it had at least afforded them the grace of monopolizing their thoughts, their anguish. They staggered, they twisted their ankles in the sand and on the gravel. They routed before them sullen armies of crabs. Suddenly, as if stricken by some abrupt inspiration, Dorn seized Shai by the arms and firmly, without saying a word, prevented him from walking a step farther.

But Shai had no need of explanations: the shade was alive; it whispered with malefic presence. *There!*

Behind an outcrop of stone, a rocky arm thrust into the spume, figures manifested themselves.

The pirates.

Indeed, the pirates. It was wrong ever to have trusted they had fallen dormant upon their past victories. They were like the shadows or the plague: they returned the moment the light lessened or the mind began to wander. More greedy, more heinous than before.

Messengers of destiny.

Shai tried to pierce the darkling shade with his eyes. It looked as if a thick black cloak had just fallen between the sea and the shore, a surreal camouflage shielding the incursions of these pillagers. As if they had conjured it by witchery and misdeed, the unnameable powers of the night.

The pirate craft came unforeseen and sudden as birds of prey. They deployed themselves swiftly, taking with reckless ease a route straight across the water. Silent. Sullen. Since the Horde had established itself in proximity to the sea, they had changed their tactics: their raids were no longer accompanied by a warlike din: prudent and efficient, they rose out of the darkness and orchestrated their strikes with an almost diabolical accuracy.

"There are at least two hundred of them," said Shai, "and they're between us and the camp. What can we do?"

Dorn chuckled. "What do you expect? Nothing. Just hold still and wait for them to finish what they've come to do. If you try anything, you'll die."

Shai hid himself behind the rocks. His hand clutched the blaster like an amulet, a potent charm against these apparitions in the dark. The weapon was ready, impatient to hurl death. Orange, miniature suns, in devastating bursts.

Suns of dread, suns of death in an ocean of darkness.

They deployed themselves silently, trying to keep the pebbles from rattling under their feet. Motionless, their confused shapes broken by the irregular fractures of the night, the pirate ships resembled beasts in hypocritical slumber.

The pirates directed themselves toward the dunes, toward the labyrinth of hillocks which barely defended the first mountainous barriers of the hinterland. Shai had never understood why the men of the coast defended themselves so poorly against the incursions of the pirates. Of course they lived entirely on the take from their nets and it was unthinkable for them to withdraw too far from the rocky bows and inlets where they moored their boats, but they might have regrouped, raised fortifications behind which they might have retired at nightfall.

They would surely have been able to post guards, to build watch towers, in fine to establish an entire system of defense to complicate life for the plunderers. The fear of reprisals, the dread of increasing the fury of the pirates restrained them; the tactical, if not numerical, superiority of the pirates did not explain it all. There was about these pitiless reavers a sort of superstitious aura: they possessed powers which rendered them invincible, even invulnerable. The shamans in any case peddled these rumors, affirming that the pirates possessed a drug which they consumed before going to battle, a drug which cured the most grievous wounds. Others spoke of a sort of salve with which they coated their bodies, the effects of which were truly miraculous. Bearface, who had no love of shamans, maintained that all such rumors were meant only to keep the people of the coast in a climate of supernatural dread, so that they might continue to pay without striking so much as a blow the monstrous tribute which the pirates considered as their due. *These village sorcerers have allied themselves with the corsairs. An arrangement which permits them to rule by fear on the one hand and derive countless prerogatives from that superstition, and on the other permits certain ones to play their ancient role as hidden directors of the community. If I had my way, I'd hang a few of their shamans by the heels, head down into the fire, just long enough to make them confess their treachery, no, I'd leave them on the beach staked out by all fours, I'd smear their privates with rancid grease. The touch of the first crab would have them singing like a flock of nightingales.*

There were still two sentries out on the dunes. They warmed their hands and their bellies at a wood fire. When the pirates rose out of the darkness they immediately took to their heels, screaming. They did not get far: whip cords coiled about their legs and they plunged headlong, groaning, with ludicrous wavings of their arms. The dreadful gurgling sounds which arose then, in that darkness teeming with presences, were significant: the sentries had just been murdered.

"One can't just let them do this," said Shai. "We have to stop them from reaching the village."

"Be still," Dorn growled. "We'll slip along

the rocks and rejoin the Horde. Then we'll come back and . . ."

"By then it'll be too late. They'll have killed, raped people—and they'll have escaped with their slaves—"

Now the night resounded with cries and howls, mad lights danced: the pirates had invaded the village, scaled the crude palisade, more symbol than barrier, which defended the approach. (A detail which deserves telling: in the morning the survivors discovered the body of an attacker in the enclosure. He had miscalculated his speed, for he had impaled himself on a stake which projected a few inches beyond the serrate line of the palisade. The expression on his face was the caricature of a demon: hate transformed the features of the corpse in a monstrous and repulsive fashion. The rays of the sun as they slanted down on him made his teeth shine like the teeth of a beast of prey. His lips drawn back, he looked as if he were trying even in death to sink his teeth into phantom attackers. Logic would have indicated to the survivors who clustered closely around the twisted corpse that here were posed certain essential questions on the alleged invulnerability of the pirates, but instead, the villagers began all at once to whine and babble in fear. Seeing which, the shaman, eager to turn the course of events to his own advantage, hastened to create a diversion by thundering forth a lengthy deathchant. A few acolytes then lifted the corpse of the impaled pirate, rolled it in a blanket and hurled it, under the attentive eye of the shaman, into a ditch which already contained the pitiful remains of a score of villagers.)

"Do what you wish," Shai exclaimed, "but you can't let—"

The sound of his voice lost itself in the reddening shadows. Dorn tried to say something to stop him then as he darted out into the night, the laser pistol unholstered in a somewhat theatrical gesture, but things were going too fast. They unfurled beyond the protagonists like a film gone out of phase.

Dorn wrapped himself in a gust of smoke, while his very voice became insubstantial, and Shai, continuing his charge, penetrated into the burning village, involved right in the course of the attackers. Training his weapon on those who rushed to right and to left of him, he enveloped no few of them in an aureole of fire before they discovered him. A blade pierced his arm, a cord whipped about his right ankle, biting and burning his flesh, his throat filled his fire, his eyes teared in an acrid smoke that smelled of dead flesh, and he fell back, choked with anger and with fear, pain exploding at the four extremities of his body.

Dorn—Lsi—Bearface!
Orange fire. Twisted faces. Maws of gaping flame.

Bearface was wakened at the edge of dawn by a brutal hand which grasped his shoulder.
"Hetman! Hetman! They've come back!"
Rapid as weasels with the scent of blood, a few shreds of nightmare swept the screen of Bearface's mind.
"Who is it?" he demanded in a confused voice while his hand, quite by instinct, was groping for the handle of his battle axe.
"It's me, hetman, Kjul!"
Bearface's hand stopped its furtive movement. Kjul, who had shared with him so many adventures and misadventures, triumphs and calamities, was one of his best warriors. And he had come to love this man as a brother.
"Pirates! They've wounded Dorn and taken Shai—"
"The dogs! The damned dogs!"
The nightmarish flickers had become letters of fire, and the message they wrote across Bearface's soul and reddened eyes had become the realization of a merciless reality. With a brutal gesture, Bearface shoved Kjul back, cast him sprawling on the wool carpet.
"Hetman!"

"I should never have let him go to the cliffs! The boy is too implusive!"

"You couldn't sit on him like a hen on an egg."

"Shut up, Kjul. That you're my best warrior doesn't give you the authority to contradict me today. Hold your tongue."

The man whose features were those of a bear blazed with an anger greater than nature. His flesh convulsed in an access of pain. He suffered as an animal suffers from whom one has reft its young; he suffered a pain without mitigation, brutal as the breaking of a storm.

"And the little one—does she know?"

"Not yet, hetman. You were the first. No one before you—"

"That's good, that's good— Gather my warriors! All of them. And tell the women of my house to take care of Lsi."

The serpent of white metal, outlined in pale fires, undulated in endless coils: its emerald eyes plunged needles of acid ice into Shai's eyes. The pain which flowed from that attack was fierce, persistent. It flowed in little prickling waves down to his groin. He suffered.

A howl escaped his twisted mouth, and someone very far away in the heights of the metallic night where the serpent still danced its ballet of death spoke.

"He's coming to, Captain-pasha."

"That's good. If he'd died, I'd have made you pay very dear for it."

"He has a tough hide, Captain-pasha. In a little while he'll be all yours . . . and you can interrogate him."

Shai slowly mounted toward a shining glass. He lay on his back and let himself drift upward in a liquid, blue-walled spiral. It was a gentle, if somewhat disquieting ascent, but he was powerless against the current which swept him thus upward to the pale metallic heights. To his great astonishment the emerald-eyed serpent had vanished.

He opened his eyes as something shook at him more and more brutally: perhaps it was a succession of waves washing over his body to push him to the beach . . . or toward the open sea. Gripped by panic, he tried to rise in this sluggish liquid: a hand left the center of the glass (or the metallic night) and descended to rest on his chest.

"Calm down," said a whistling voice, "don't waste your strength. You're going to need it."

He realized then that he was in a cabin on one of the pirate ships. He remembered the battle and his capture in the midst of flames and the riot of looting.

The one they called Captain-pasha leaned above him, his eyes aglow with amusement.

He looked a bit like a rat, with his long face, his pointed nose, his grizzled hair which was starting to thin. In spite of his clothing which maintained a studied elegance, the jewels which adorned exceeding long fingers and the manner in which his nails had been cut and polished, one could surmise that this man was brutal and gross.

Three daggers of differing length were thrust through his large belt of red leather. They were bizarrely worked, and their hilts of semi-precious metals suggested obscene shapes.

The other man, the one who stood behind Shai, out of the limits of his sight, let slip a small sort of chuckle. "You ought to pay your respects to our Captain-pasha."

The Captain-pasha waved his hand impatiently. "That's enough," he said, "enough clowning about." He leaned forward more and his too-delicate hands came to rest on Shai's shoulders. If snakes had hands, Shai thought, their touch could not be much different from— But his mind betrayed him, and he thought suddenly of all those he left behind him, of their anguish—

"You're the leader of the pirates," he said. "Why am I not dead?"

"To tell the truth," the other grinned, "I had the intention of interrogating you, not of answering your questions." He sighed a long sigh, caressing one of his daggers. "It is true," he declared, in a falsely quiet tone, "that impertinence is the privilege of youth. I let you live because you're not of an age to die. And particularly because you know certain things I need to learn from your own lips."

The cabin round about them reflected the expensive tastes of the Captain-pasha. All about them lay precious bric-a-brac and carved chests, gleaming furs and rich cushions.

"You do have an interest in demonstrating your cooperation. Your life hangs by the merest thread, and I can break that thread at any instant I choose. I don't have any reputation for patience—right, Foskus?"

"They even say you're rather *im*patient . . . but I'm sure that our young friend will do himself the favor of going along with us. After all—in his situation, he has everything to gain by cooperating."

"Well, well, Foskus, but you really don't need to go into detail. We'll see to all that in due time. For the moment, I want you to take a look at our guest's wounds. One or the other of them just could get infected."

Foskus came into his full view and Shai was surprised at his beauty. Because of the coarseness of his voice and the threats he had offered, he had imagined under those influences a man grossly hewn, heavily built, inclined to the most extreme brutalities. Instead there came into his view an athlete with well-defined muscles, gray eyes, whose somewhat soft mouth had perhaps something of femininity. Shai understood all at once with the instinct of those accustomed to danger, that of the two men who stood before him, Foskus was by far the most pitiless and the most cruel. It would be difficult to escape from him once he had gotten it into his head that he wanted your hide, and as for tricking him, there could certainly be no question of that.

"Let me see that," he said, drawing aside the torn and bloody garments which hung lamentably from Shai's body. "Huh. More frightened than hurt, Captain-pasha. A dagger thrust. A few whip marks. In a few days there'll be no trace."

"You hear that, my young friend?" said the Captain-pasha. "In a few days you'll be in excellent health, ready to enjoy life; and life on our archipelago is not life elsewhere. It's true life. Yes, you could hardly put it better than that. True life. Or, well, then, there's hell. As you will; you choose. Good. Foskus, take good care of him. Salve and tea, and anything you want."

Foskus' hands were caressing him with a quite mesmerizing gentleness.

"Quite a doctor, isn't he?" asked the Captain-pasha. "And what strength he hides in those fingers! You feel it . . . you feel it as he works, how he handles you?"

"Yes," said Shai, "I feel it." (Fear had lodged in his voice, ready to leap out, furious and fuming.)

"The shaman yonder—" The finely manicured hand gestured widely in an ill-defined direction. "—told me about you, about you and the others who live in the fortified camp. It appears you are famous warriors. And you, they claim that you're a veritable wellspring of science. You could become someone . . . I mean someone really powerful. The shamans in general don't like you much; they find you're a young fluff, too intelligent to be honest. If you see what I mean. I don't give a fig what the shamans think of you, but they are very useful to me. Thanks to them, or rather, thanks to their power over the people of the Coast, I carry on my little traffic in slaves without having to fret myself. Ah, yes, life was beautiful before your arrival in these regions." Captain-pasha sighed yet again from the depths of his heart. He rubbed his chin and went on. "You like to smoke?"

"I don't know. That depends," Shai said, slowly, as if he searched for words. "If you— want—"

"The herb is good. Better than the weed. It

puts dark thoughts to flight. The legend has it that it banishes death—for a while. The herb is sweet and good—"

Captain-pasha came to lean once again over Shai, put a long cigarette between his lips. A flame leapt, bluish, and the smoke insinuated itself down Shai's throat.

"My name is Malaoud," said the Captain-pasha. "We have to understand one another, you and I, young man. You have to learn to think sensibly, my boy, for around here the good do die young."

Foskus's hands and the smoke of the herb—

The rolling of the ship. Slow, mournful. It was good to let oneself be carried away, not to think any longer about useless things, painful things, comfortable things. A gigantic motion rocked the world.

What did the zealots of the Great Serpent say? The priests? That the world was flat. A sort of formidable disk floating on a shadow-sea. When one went outside the limits of the world—what happened when one trespassed beyond the limits of this flat world?

Vertigo.

One could do nothing against the wave which rocked the sea. Nothing. Except let oneself go.

The Archipelago. Shai had often wondered what the pirates' lair must look like and especially

whether it was as unassailable as people claimed
it was. He was surprised to discover that they
had hardly exaggerated in calling it a natural
fortress. The Rocky Isles (there were seven of
them, besides several reefs of less import) looked
like unassailable citadels so well set in the sea
that it looked as if it would take a massed
army of some twenty thousand men to get the
better of them.

Standing between Malaoud and Foskus, Shai
gazed outward as they neared the imposing
rock wall which defended the access of Dja-
maidah port.

"This is the capital," said Captain-pasha;
"you'll see that it's quite the equal of all your
fortresses and your citadels put together. We've
created a perfect State. All pirates here are
equal, and the chiefs, since we have to have
them to carry on our trade, are chosen for as
many years as they show themselves worthy of
that command. Myself, I've been Captain-pasha
for . . . for how long, Foskus?"

Shai hardly heard Malaoud's chatter. He was
reflecting bitterly that he was in a trap; that
no one would come to rescue him. The men of
the Coast had only small forces at their disposal,
and the Horde was damned to helplessness,
stranded on that shore, incapable of crossing
the waters to come deal with these invaders.
Even if they had had at their command the

ships essential to such a mission of revenge, would they not be cruelly shattered upon this uncrossable barrier, would they not be repulsed again and again, decimated? The Horde was not well-armed enough to assail these natural, cyclopean defenses, and it was composed of warriors accustomed to fight upon terra firma and most particularly standing in their stirrups.

Foskus's hand came to rest on Shai's shoulder as Magnus' hand had rested once and long ago. The young man saw in that a sort of omen, but he was quite incapable of interpreting it in any coherent fashion.

He was presently thinking of Lsi, and his heart ached with sadness. A heavy, burning sadness which rained acid into his vitals.

The house of the Captain-pasha Malaoud stood in the very center of the capital, in a street exceeding large and bordered with strange coniferous trees. This was the quarter of the city reserved for select ones of the officers. All the residences looked alike in deference to the pirates' democratic theories, very much alike. Only one house surpassed the others in height and beauty, with its ornate façade of mosaics and bas-relief, its heiratic colonnades; and someone told him that this was the residence of the Admiral.

"The Admiral is very old," Malaoud added,

"but that's not of any particular importance, for his title is entirely an honorific."

"I'd like to ask you a question, Captain-pasha," said Shai, as they drew near the officer's residence.

"Only one?"

"Only one, Captain-pasha."

"I'm listening, my lad. Do try to be concise: we're almost there."

"Why do you treat me so well? My place is among the conquered, the slaves. That's your law; no bargainings, no favoritism, everyone for the chain and the whip—"

Foskus's hand seized Shai's nape and began to close upon it painfully, with a frightful application and doggedness. *He's going to break my spine.*

"You don't talk in that tone, hear?"

"Let be, Foskus. —I really didn't get the drift of your question, Shai, and it does seem to me it was rather awkwardly put. . . . Perhaps you'd like to repeat that—in different words."

Two beautiful black-skinned women emerged from the house and came up on either side of them as they walked up. They cast Shai looks from beneath their brows.

"Your question will have to wait. Here are my two housekeepers, Aella and Zaphyria. Two lovely names and two lovely whores, my friend, I give you my word on it."

The black women who bore the names of Aella and Zaphyria wore voluminous jeweled robes which set off the dark majesty of their flesh.

They were truly beautiful as sin.

But their laughter seemed forced, very like the Captain-pasha's cordiality, underlain with secret understandings.

Shai lay full length on the warm paving-stones, as one of the black-skinned women, she whose prenomen was Zaphyria, busied herself in anointing him with a thin salve. Whenever she leaned forward to deliver a long stroke, her beautiful pear-shaped breasts shook and jumped wonderfully.

"You're lucky," she said suddenly, "to have pleased the Captain-pasha. To him we're only beasts."

He knew not what to answer her, disquieted by what possibilities could suddenly arise to break the false order of this day.

"Beware," Zaphyria murmured, leaning her right hand upon his belly, "the plague in this house is Dr. Foskus. That man is leprous." And she added, with a little crease of her brows: "He's a witch and he allies himself with demons. When he speaks, it's hell itself that speaks through his mouth. The Captain-pasha swears not save by him and refuses him nothing. All the house lies at Foskus's feet."

In the course of her words, the young woman leaned on his belly with such force that he groaned.

"Oh. Excuse me. I hurt you."

"No," he said, a little disarrayed, "you surprised me." Shai avoided the black woman's eyes because the situation began to make him anxious and because the nearness of that three-quarters naked flesh set the blood to beating in his temples. Only a little wrap of yellow silk concealed Zaphyria's groin. Her presence recalled to him his first experience of sex in the house of women, and he found it harder and harder to conceal his distress. He tried to take another tack in a sudden change of subject.

"Zaphyria, have you ever seen the man they call the Admiral?"

The young woman leaned over him in confidentiality, so close now that the tips of her breasts began to press gently on Shai's chest. A capricious twinkle danced in the eyes of the black woman, and her generous lips parted on shining teeth. "He's an old man who never goes out of his great house. They say that he—well, they say that he's committed more murders in his life than all the captains combined. Anyhow there's one thing I do know: the admiral is the one who governs the slave trade. He decides everything in that department, and though you never see him in the town, he knows everything that happens."

She shook her head as if to give emphasis to her words, began a phrase, then, in a change of mind, she set herself again to anoint Shai's limbs.

"You please me very much," she murmured, her eyes fixed on Shai's, "it's been so long since someone affected me the way you do. Life is short, for we are all in the hand of a cruel god. Before I was a black whore, I owned a vast estate yonder, the other side of the sea; and countless servants waited on me and deferred to me." She lay down upon the stones beside the young man. "You think I lie to make myself interesting. A black whore could never have reigned over a province—could she?"

He gave her no answer but to put his hands on her. "Why do you talk that way?" he asked.

The next morning they led him before Captain-pasha Malaoud. For the occasion the Captain-pasha was surrounded by some of his peers, all richly dressed and armed with parade sabers and with splendidly worked daggers. Foskus, constantly smiling, was likewise in evidence. He stood with an affected deference, behind his master's seat.

"Approach, young man," said Malaoud. "My

friends, behold the lad I told you of. His name is Shai, and my informants have forewarned me: he is intelligent and full of tricks. And certainly more than a little presumptuous. But his youth must convince you to show yourselves merciful—"

He kept on in that way for some few minutes, sometimes losing himself in his byzantine phrases. Then, suddenly, with that brusqueness which Shai had already seen in him, he shifted manners.

"Listen," he cried, "you have seen the garden side of this existence; now you must make acquaintance with the territory of shadow and horror!" And turning himself toward the other captains: "Before we interrogate him," he said, "I think that it would be interesting and profitable to have him visit the quarries of Jathral. A glance at the geological wonders of that district will certainly draw tears of passion from him."

A sparse brief laughter greeted this proposal.

Dipping into a terra cotta vessel, silent slaves served the captains and Foskus a sort of very murky beer. The silence went on while the officers drank long drafts. Foskus declined with a grandiloquent gesture when one offered to refill his goblet. Manifestly he had no wish to muddle his thinking. His gray eyes gleamed, and nothing escaped them.

"We would like to learn from you a certain number of practical things. For example, how many men your hetman has under his command and the manner in which the defenses of your camp are arranged. I see that makes you angry. No one likes to betray his own kind. So we will be as patient. Not too long. For as I have told you, patience is not numbered among my virtues. . . . We will leave you a little time for reflection. After you have visited the quarries of Jathral, you will have all night and all day to make your decision."

This is my punishment, Shai thought. *The first treason I committed decided my destiny, and now I am placed in such a dilemma that—* The faces of his friends passed before his eyes, like ghosts on parade. Lsi, the hetman, Dorn, who was perhaps already dead, all the rest of them . . . they were haggard, ragged, bloodied. They fixed upon him the gaze of their dead eyes. And that gaze pierced him through and through.

The screams were not audible from this distance but the stink was frightful. It rose to heaven in moist, appalling waves; it devoured all space, it enveloped everything like a flight of locusts or funereal butterflies whose eager tongues lusted to drink of blood-hued calixes.

This fetor made Shai stagger. Foskus held him by the arm, still full of concern.

"This is nothing, my friend, nothing. The best is yet to come."

Then the cries and the wails began. When they were no more than a few hundred paces from the famous quarries of Jathral. Never had Shai heard such a cacophony, never in his most awful dreams had he imagined such a variety of sounds. He felt himself plunged into a churning sea, an unfurling of unbearable music. These cries and these lamentations formed an arrhythmical skein of brutal flourishes, a swelling of unbearable volume.

"In the ancient tongue Jathral means Depth. In the specific case of the quarries, it evidently takes on a quite symbolic application. You'll understand in a moment."

They finally reached the edge of the crevasse, an ax-blow in the rock, a crack in solid stone. At the bottom of this hole, which was difficult to judge whether it was of natural origin or whether man had fashioned it over the course of years, confused shapes went to and fro wreathed in pestilential fog.

"You see," said Foskus, "Captain-pasha Malaoud was right. Nothing is as good as life experience. To tell you some vague tale— But why should I waste words? Look. *Look!*"

Foskus's hand had become brutal, a veritable vise. It bent him dangerously toward the abyss.

"We have given you a choice. Between the company of the Captain-pasha and his women and this descent into Jathral. A night and a day of reflection—that should quite suffice you."

Shai wept. He shut his eyes under the assault of the pain, but curiosity was strong. His lids, slowly, inexorably, lifted.

And discovered a quivering mass covered the bottom of the pit with a kind of putrifying mosaic. Zombies so ragged one could not tell if they were still on this world or whether they had returned from the other to accomplish their unspeakable tasks.

Someone laughed above Shai's head.

Whispered faint and mocking words.

Later when he had recovered his wits, the young man realized it was only a bird.

"In the ancient tongue—(what cursed tongue?) Jathral means depth, abysm, sewer.... Be very careful not to fall into that open maw where death parades its most solemn robes, fringed with filth, bordered with blood. We give you a choice. You are blessed among the blessed, Shai, for we have given you the choice between life and death. Those you see down there no longer have a choice."

A strident wail rose from that frightful gehenna. In spite of his revulsion, he leaned forward, clinging to the rocky excrescences. A hot breath began to beat against his face like the membranous wings of some hellish raptor.

He wanted to see who cried out so, in the torments of hell. He wanted to know. . . .

Foskus's hand was there, more gentle now. A friendly hand, which protected him against any loss of equilibrium.

The men who came and went in the quarries of Jathral all looked alike: the privations and the sufferings had turned their skin to leather till they were no more than strange things of flaccid leather, corroded by the heat, the putrid emanations, the assaults of eternal pestilences, the daily bites of the whip.

"I don't understand," said Shai. "You have the custom of exacting as much money as you can from your captives. Why have you put these men into this pit?"

"You don't understand anything, do you? You're only a poor young Barbarian who has read a few books and had two or three chats with philosophers. To begin with, these men are extracting a precious substance from the rock: mendionite, a substance the uses of which are manifold; and when they are three quarters dead, they go on suffering, dying, screaming without end . . . to maintain the legend of our invincible cruelty. There's nothing like such legends to establish the power of a nation. It's politics. It takes a lot of perfume to cover the stink of politics."

Shai scarcely heard Foskus's words. Leaning perilously above the gulf he was exploring its anfractuosities, green, purple, stained with indigo. The cry persisted even now: "*AAaaaaa*". A guttural lament which seemed torn from the depths of an ironworks. And he finally caught sight of the one who cried out so in the enormity of his suffering: two guards clad in metal and leather, faces protected by filter-masks, were in the act of flogging him to death. They tore red runnels in that blemished flesh, a lacery of scarlet stripes.

"Why? Why?" stammered the young man.

"For you, my lad, and on the express order of our all-seeing admiral!"

His wits scattered on the wide winds, but he could not escape from the reek which came from the charnelhouse of rebel slaves. His feet sunk in the sand, he scanned the horizon as if he hoped there to see a great fleet with flags flying, headed for the pirates' lair.

With the end of his staff he traced in the wet sand an isoceles triangle. Then he wrote at its three corners a series of capital letters. When he had finished his labor he was surprised at what he had obtained. What dark voice had breathed that craziness into him?

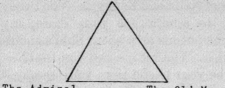

Dr. Pfeil

The Admiral   The Old Man of the Cliff

A gentle voice tore him from his meditations and he turned suddenly to find himself face to face with Foskus.

"Making plans for your escape?" the intruder asked, in a tone which pretended to be casual.

"No one can escape from this island," Shai replied. "You said so yourself."

Foskus broke into laughter. "That's so. But you are crazy enough to risk your brilliant future in this feckless enterprise."

Everywhere I go, I meet enigmatic old men. They live very far from one another but they all play a part in my destiny. Perhaps they're only coincidences, but too many coincidences, they say, finally eliminate all chance.

"How was the view?"

The young man shivered. He almost asked stupidly: "What view?" —then he cried: "Is that the fate you hold out to me if I—run?"

Foskus's gray eyes shone with honeyed sweetness. "Why such a question? Have you really the intention of deserting our company?" And without leaving Shai time to answer, he added: "The caresses of Aella and Zaphyria—don't they do anything to ameliorate your exile, my friend?" Foskus put his arm about Shai's shoulders and smiled. "You let me call you that?"

"Better to be your friend than your enemy."

With slow persistence, Foskus's right boot began to erase the geometric figure.

IV

THE SUBTERFUGUES OF DR. PFEIL

"Well, young Shai," asked Captain-pasha Malaoud, "have we had a good day . . . I mean, an instructive trip?"

No reply.

The Captain-pasha knit his brows. "Your silence saddens me, my lad. Would you feel yourself lacking something? Perhaps Zaphyria and Aella haven't given you all the service you should rightly expect of them? Foskus, my dear Foskus, would you have let a few hours of inattention slip from your sense of duty, would you have neglected our friend Shai for these last few hours?"

"No, no, my dear lord," Foskus exclaimed, "absolutely not, but I do believe the stress of the day has temporarily deprived him of words."

There was a new silence, during which spurts of water splashed into the pools of the winter garden. In spite of the wafts of perfume Shai's nostrils were still filled with the stink of Jathral. His throat was still constricted with fear, to be sure, but part of it was hatred, red and hot as a spurt of blood.

"That thing yonder, on the island, is terrible," he said finally, "terrible. They beat a prisoner to death. They cut him to ribbons with their whips."

"Sit down. You're overwrought. I'm going to have them bring you a cup of wine. Maybe you ought to smoke a bit, just to get your thoughts in order ... I'm only thinking about what's best for you. I adore intelligent lads, lads with bright futures. And what future could you dream of among those bastard curs that comprise your hetman's horde? Listen. I know you have a lady friend. If we win, with your help—nothing will happen to her. You can't play the hero, you know. You're at the age for heroical and desperate gestures ... but here we are, Foskus and I, to guide you, to give you useful advice. Even the Admiral is interested in you. The Admiral is a paragon of wisdom. He knows all, understands all, sees all—and now—Drink!"

A slave had come in carrying a platter with

a tall carafe and exceedingly tall footed glasses, like herons balancing themselves on one leg. The wine was fruity, potent. It must have come from beyond the sea. Perhaps. . . .

The whole cruel business mustn't happen here, again. Of what are we the playthings, the toys? Perhaps it would be better to let go. . . . To be silent. To let myself be thrown into that stinking hole, to be torn by the whips of masked, cuirassed torturers, impersonal as death's own slaves. Perhaps. . . .

A distant voice hissed in his head like the sputtering of a candle about to gutter out.

"Don't tremble so," whispered Foskus. "You still have time before you, to reflect upon your decision. Here, smoke this fine herb."

Shai defended himself with a limp hand. In vain. The wafts of the drug penetrated the secret caverns of his soul. He slipped yet again into an ocean whose slow waves, almost like a painted ocean, attested a suspect oiliness. There appeared a black profile portrait like an image cut from some old book. When the turgid waters closed above his head a music sounded: tambours, flutes, cymbals. More distant, trumpets, and uncommon in this concert, foghorns, as if ships were sailing toward the archipelago. But he knew that this was impossible.

A man with three heads stood motionless upon the sill of a cyclopean doorway, open upon a high wall. His triple stare was set upon Shai and his three mouths spoke in chorus. "We have no time to waste," said the three mouths of this apparition. "We've tested you with patience and extreme forbearance. The hour has come when you must choose our side, the glory of our cause."

The first head was that of Dr. Denner Pfeil.

The second head was that of the old man of the cliff.

The third head, which must logically belong to the Admiral, was only a white skull with two deepset coals for eyes. And a thin mouth which spoke in unison with its two companions.

"I know what you feel," said Aella, "we were noble once, before we were snatched from our homelands, from our friends, from our people. Now we are two marish whores subject to the whims of the lords of the Archipelago."

They were both lying in Shai's bed and pressing themselves gently against the young man. Like elder sisters, more experienced, already heavy with wisdom and regret.

"If the Admiral were *really* interested in you," Zaphyria declared, "you would never escape by lies or tricks. It seems that—"

"—he knows everything, understands everything, sees everything," Shai interrupted her with a voice filled with bitterness. "I already heard that from the Captain-pasha and the doctor."

The two women were warm and perfumed against him. The nearness of their skin disturbed him in spite of his morose thoughts, his pricklings of fear. Aella's right hand rested on his chest; Zaphyria's left hand gently pressed upon his navel.

"This frightful crevasse yonder, all this suffering," he moaned. "I can't believe—"

"Don't think about it . . . try. We'll help you, Aella and I."

Aella's mouth came to rest upon his lips, hot and moist as a fruit and filled with potent moisture, while Zaphyria's hand descended to his groin and encircled his sex. The night was filled with rustlings, furtive glidings, as if silken serpents had broken into the shadowy room where but a few small braziers burned, in which the two women had but lately cast perfumes.

Aella's tongue was expert and gentle, and such was the skill of Zaphyria's fingers that Shai's heart began to throb like a war drum. His arms drew the two women close. Phosphenes burst beneath his eyelids, waves swelled in his gut. Memories perished in this silent sea of pleasure. In vain he sought to raise in his memory Lsi's features, or those of Bearface. Something had broken in him, but it was impossible for him under the circumstances to feel remorse for his infidelity. The storm came with red and viscous waves, irrepressible. He cried out, his mouth buried in Zaphyria's shoulder . . . if it was not Aella's.

Later, when Aella and Zaphyria had utterly exhausted him, drained him of strength and cradled him like a babe in their arms, between their breasts, their thighs, he fell into deep slumber. Where his terrors returned to him, crackling like icy blue flame: the door was there again. And so was the wall, now crowned with rolling columns of smoke. Then the tricephalic monster rose up in a spitting of tiny orange sparks. But this time its three heads were the heads of women.

The first was Aella's.

The second was Lsi's.

The third was Zaphyria's.

Lsi's eyes ran with slow, blood-red tears, but the eyes of Aella and Zaphyria stayed dry, half hidden behind the fringe of lashes and the rampart of their lids.

The effect produced by these three women's heads mounted on an old man's body was grotesque and monstrous. Especially since the brain was totally naked now and afflicted with a vast member, a vastly swollen scrotum.

The heads that were Aella and Zaphyria began to insult that which was Lsi's. And the bleeding eyes continued to weep their red tears. While the brain underwent a monstrous erection.

When he waked, bathed in sweat, between the two women who remained deep in slumber, he tried in vain to interpret the meaning of this nightmare.

The Admiral's house was bathed in a sulfurous light. The sun struggled painfully across a barrier of cloud. The yellow banner, charged with a double-headed eagle and two daggers crossed below by the blade of a third, drooped somewhat on its staff ... except when the wind came back, sickly and insidious.

Shai trembled. He recalled other flags flying over the fortress of his childhood: the standards and the banners of the Great Serpent.

On the porch of the admiral's residence, two gigantic guards held themselves motionless. They were clad in livery of gray, belted in red, wearing leather helms and armed with falchions and daggers.

When they met the cortege which was the Captain-pasha, Dr. Foskus, and the young man, they bowed double in a manner at first glance somewhat obsequious but which began simply to seem part of the manner hereabouts.

"The admiral awaits you," said the doorkeeper. "Do go in."

The valves turned on their hinges without

the least noise, and they entered into the silent house.

Rarely had Shai seen a room as barren as the hall of the admiralty. It looked to him a little like the dormitories of his childhood, the refectories and the testing-rooms of the fortress. He had expected (and he did not know why) a setting of luxury, a show of sumptuousness. Instead he felt as if he had entered the retreat of some hermit, the residence of an anchorite.

Oddly enough this discovery chilled him to the marrow.

This rigor and this nakedness rendered the inhabitant of these places more menacing, even less human.

By the high windows the yellow daylight made a weary entrance. They kept walking, preceded by one of the door wardens; they crossed rooms empty or virtually so, where their steps echoed long, like lamentations. Facing a little door of white metal, the little troop stopped, still without a word uttered, gripped in an almost religious intensity.

If I talk now, Shai thought, *I shall abort my destiny. I shall damn myself to death.*

The guardian of the door rapped with his fist against the wood. Three times. Then he waited.

The door opened on its own. Gaped slowly upon a suspect shadow.

They entered, but the guard stayed outside

the room, while the door closed itself in muf-
fled softness.

"Welcome," said the personage who wished
himself known as the Admiral.

Shai struggled now against an overwhelm-
ing tide of panic. And yet the man who came to
meet them had nothing of the repugnant or
frightening about him. He was a great lord
with waxen features, with extremely thin lips,
and his blue eyes shone with vivid force. He
made one think of a Doctor of the Temple of
the Great Serpent, but his face had not the
harshness which usually marked the zealots of
the Great Serpent. On the contrary, his eyes
rested upon Shai with an infinite gentleness, a
kind of solemn good will. With a wide and
gracious gesture he directed his visitors to mats
placed side by side on the floor.

"I am happy to see you here, in this house,
Shai."

Shai opened his mouth to give a polite answer to the old man's salutations, but his companions gripped the flesh of his forearms and
he understood at the last moment that he must
hold his peace.

"You come from far away. If my information
is correct, you have been following a hetman
with the face of a bear, since the time you gave
him the keys of a fortress. Some would call
that act treason. Others would name it an act

of justice. I would rather not debate morals with you. Every man can interpret the truth in his own way . . . up to a certain point. Here for example, verity is better defined. In the sense that it belongs to everyone and to no one in ordinary time, and to me alone in time of war."

Shai understood suddenly that this man's friendliness was pretense, that all the honey which flowed from his mouth was a rotten juice, a corruption of words, meaningless under their apparent logic. He must expect nothing from his justice. Nothing.

"We have here a somewhat peculiar regime. You must have remarked it. A sort of compromised democracy. Tempered, one might say. My friends have let you view the stinking abysses of Jathral and you had the chance to see that gehenna. But they also let you taste the pleasures, the very distracting pleasures (the term is somewhat inadequate, you will grant me that)—in the company of that delightful pair of odalisques, Zaphyria and Aella. You must now make a choice, for your friends do begin to worry us a little. What shall we do on this rocky land without our surely reprehensible but profitable—slave trade?"

"If I may be permitted," said Foskus, cutting off the admiral in midword with shocking casualness, "I shall make clear to your Excellency that this boy seems to maintain scruples which may be quite ... deeply rooted. But it goes without saying that we have lessoned him long and properly. Now he knows all the advantages and the inconveniences of his situation."

"Good, good!" cried the admiral, "that does let us speak clearly."

Roving hands came to torment Shai's half-sleep.

The admiral's mouth opened, quivered gently till it took the shape of an ophidian oval and clipped out these words:

"We have had—we have always had—a dire need of you. Messages have come to us telling us that you were a terrible young man, that you would trouble destiny in all its ramifications. Go back to the beginning of the way, Shai. Try to comprehend."

The admiral drew backward, chuckling, his eyes like ivory, his nostrils dilating.

"Fortunately, yes, fortunately, we have captain Otman. He is the eye of our conscience, my young friend. He patrols in the most forsaken territories of our subconscious. If you see what I—what we mean, what we want to say to you— Captain Otman will see you in a moment. You will meet him."

—*I'm dreaming this.*

—*Yes*, Shai thought. *I'm in a dream. In a moment the light will come back and I won't*

*have a thing to say. No more. OR YOU'RE
TALKING NONSENSE!*

The moving hands invaded Shai's sleep, turning the stuff of his dreams to stone.

The admiral's eyes glittered in the shadow.

Captain Otman knocked on the door of the office.

The guardians gave him passage and bowed to him.

Captain Otman: his hands were gloved in raw silk and his face was masked in the most glittering crystal.

Foskus's hands, insidious, caressed Shai from the limit of his belly to his diaphragm.

A fierce music sounded. Notes scattered in the distance.

The guards let in Captain Otman. And the Captain-pasha bowed before the newcomer. "Take him away, take him away without delay, we weary of him!"

The hand of this Captain Otman lifted, chasing some slow-moving fireflies. "Orders are orders." His mask glittered in the dark; the windows through which his gaze passed seemed to contain a fire yet more difficult to bear.

Foskus's hands pushed Shai gently toward the newcomer. Captain Otman spoke behind his crystal mask and his words came but slowly and a little deformed to the young man's ears.

"You must . . . Shai . . . take your place . . . not among these barbarians, these . . . poor soiled . . . dogs. Among us, you will have. . . ." The crystal mask caught a few drops of liquid light, quivered in the supercharged atmosphere of the mysterious room. "I've received a new reprieve from the admiral. Because . . . precious knowledge, but it will be the last . . . time . . . I can't do any more . . . any more on your . . . behalf."

He let himself be led away. Vague voices surrounded him, escorting him across the city of the pirates, along port streets which were animate, luxuriant. Perfumed boughs swayed in the wind, far above his head, as if winter had never had power over the eternal flowering of their magics. Shai felt himself wandering again between deceiving reality and lying dream: reduced to the mercy of strange creatures who played with him a game with incomprehensible rules. Men and women broke into laughter as they passed, cast him gibes and obscene jokes.

Then the city noise was silenced, was no more at their backs than a distant murmur.

"You see," Captain Otman said, "we are alone now. We can talk openly."

Shai came back to full awareness and realized that he was indeed alone with the stranger. He examined this extraordinary apparition more

closely. The rich silk vestments, in their deep
folds, hid the details of a body of which Shai,
for all his curiosity, could not guess the age.
As for the crystal mask, which reflected the
rays of the sun, it disguised the voice while it
hid the facial features. The stranger was no
more than a specter risen from space or time.
Yes, Shai thought, perhaps it is a time traveler.
Do such exist, time-travelers, someone who
leaves his place in the depths of duration, who
crosses the gulfs of history, without the least
difficulty, as it were some game? The man in
the crystal mask, if he was one of those who
might move through the ages, he must be a
usual visitor in this sad era, since the inhabitants of this slice of history saluted him as one
of their own.

"Follow me," said Captain Otman. "The others will attend us shortly. Let us sit in the
shelter of the rocks and talk."

The young man was too battered down to
protest. He walked directly behind his companion, and when they had seated themselves
in a sort of path cut in the rock by wind and
weather, the stranger who wished himself
known as Captain Otman held out to him a
silver flagon.

"Drink," he said, "you have a vagrant look, a
lost look." Then he added: *I admit one must be
a bit lost . . .*

Shai drank a long draft of a burning alcohol which made his eyes start from their sockets before it suffused his chest with a delicious languor.

"I have a long tale to tell you," said Captain Otman.

V

THE MONKS

This morning she could endure no longer. The anguish had grown too strong, for the night was peopled with nightmares. She saddled her own horse and rode out of the camp in spite of the remonstrances of the guard.

"I'm suffocating," she said. "I can't stay here any longer."

Finally the officer let her pass, with the feeling that he was committing a dereliction.

It was cold weather. And gray and damp. Above the rocks hung sulfurous clouds: daybreak had not quite triumphed over the night. Lsi set spurs to her horse, which whinnied long and loud with a kind of lamentation, vexed at the descent to the deserted beach.

Shai had occupied a major place in the young woman's bad dreams: sometimes he appeared to her as a cadaver eaten by crabs, sometimes as a sort of ghost with glittering eyes. His mouth would open to say something but suddenly out of it fell insects and seaweed.

She rode as far as a rocky promontory to get the widest possible view of the sea. It was senseless and she knew it, surveying thus the wasteland of the sea like some fisherwife, like a widow— But perhaps she was a widow—now. She chased away such unquiet thoughts. *You'll see, Lsi. They won't kill him. They'll use him to get a ransom or to make us talk. They'd be stupid to kill him: that wouldn't make sense—.* In such terms the hetman had sought to reassure her. He had even taken her in his arms and held her against him for a long while, with a warmth that no one would ever have expected in a man with a bear's face. She had wept and bitten the hetman's shoulder-guard in her rage. *Aye, aye, cry, my daughter, cry and you'll live to be old.* —She suddenly felt that someone in a nearby concealment was watching her. She quickly checked to see that her arbalest and its arrows were within arms' reach.

The hetman had been wild with rage: he had led out a dozen of his men and gone to the men of the Coast.

"Your shamans are stinking beasts," he had

cried then, showing his teeth like a bear. "They traffic in fear. They sell you to the pirates and you cover them with honors to pay them for their lies. They tell you that your destiny is written in the stars, in the grains of sand, in the pebbles on the shore: they tell you that the gods have willed it so; the masters of one coast, the slaves of another! Take your shamans by the ankles and castrate them with your knives!"

The chiefs had raised loud shouts and the shamans had begun to yelp in rage. He should have treated them as they deserved. But all this show of force did no good: fear was ingrained in the bodies of the people of the Coast. They would have chosen to die rather than lay hands on one of their shamans. Sure of their might and their impunity, the sorcerers and soothsayers began to vituperate against the strangers who had brought them nothing but misery and brought down on them the wrath of the gods and the demons. Hearing that, Bearface gave orders for someone to bring him two or three of those noisemakers.

The riders entered the crowd like so many knives penetrating yielding clay and chased the howling shamans to their hetman's feet.

A murmur of consternation greeted this demonstration of authority.

"The pirates," said Bearface, "have taken Shai. This young man, I love him as if he were born of my loins. I tell you this: chattering old men, stinking old rats, I tell you this: I know your treasons, there is none of your plotting has escaped me, none of the odious bargains you have made with the brigands of the Rocky Isles. If young Shai dies, I shall stake you out on the beach after you have been smeared with rancid grease. Then we will watch it as a choice spectacle, the way the crabs will dine on your guts and your entrails."

The shamans were silent, for they had never had anyone talk to them in that way. They wondered whether it was the moment now to curse these strange bringers of curses right away or whether it was more prudent to affect a scornful silence. But the hetman did not give them time to engage in philosophical self-debate: he was in a rage such that the bloodthirst exploded in his eyes. He ordered that the sorcerers be led to camp to serve as quasi-hostages.

"We'll see, indeed we will," he cried, and his voice ruffled the feathers of the seabirds which skimmed the gray wave crests. "We will indeed see whether the future proves us right."

On that somewhat sybilline utterance, he whirled his horse about and ordered his riders to go back to camp. He boiled with rage but he realized quite well that the events which were about to unfurl would do nothing to seat his authority; on the contrary, they could well make these humble shamans martyrs to their faith.

Kill the soothsayers and the necromants? He did not think of that. In this affair he was very clearly at risk of losing face.

But how to get at the pirates? The whole horde was exiled on terra firma. A troop of riders embarked on a cockleshell fleet in the dark had no chance at all. To take the corsair hideout by force was an unthinkable enterprise, already with the principal piece in check. Aye, the hetman was out of his head with anger.

Terrible, that feeling of being watched, followed by attentive eyes the while she drove her mount toward the escarpment. She reassured herself with the thought that it was most likely some fisherman or group of fishermen, fearfully hidden in a crevice of the tumbled rocks, a folk too thoroughly terrified by the pirate attack and the riders to try anything. —Or was she deceiving herself? The kidnapping of the sorcerers—was it possible it might provoke reprisals? Even on the part of timid and profoundly superstitious creatures like these fishermen?

A dreadful feeling, as if points of invisible fire were turned upon her. Fortunately she had acquired a certain skill at arbalestery and she used the dagger with still more skill. In this half-familiar hell which the world had become, a woman learned very quickly to defend herself.

Lsi, my daughter, I am a beast that trembles in a helpless rage. A wild beast in a cage! He had taken her in his arms and had squeezed her so hard that her back bruised, her ribs were crushed. This desperate strength had suddenly troubled her.

She reached the promontory and gazed at the infinite sea, across the rocky barrier, into the distance. Behind that pale scar which was the horizon terrible things were happening at the center of which was her young lover. Tears of grief and anger rolled down her face. She stayed there, her eyes lost in that gray anonymity, spray-washed and vertiginous, until the moment the longing for Shai utterly overcame her. The wind rose suddenly, and wailed in her ears in mournful howls of leaden sound.

"You are mad, wind!" cried a flight of birds that passed the summit of the promontory. "Mad, mad, mad to bind the wind!"

She was distracted from her erotic dream by that stormy flight and scream. Suddenly pierced through by that frightful sensation of being not alone but watched by a malefic presence—she turned, the arbalest cocked. There were six of them. Motionless on the promontory, only thirty paces from her. Wearing habits of solemn sackcloth. Like ghosts. *It's impossible! We're hundreds of leagues from the fortress! And the fortress no longer exists. What are monks of the Great Serpent doing here? They were all killed in the sack of the citadel. For it would have been mad to let one of them live!*

But they were indeed there, the zealots of the Great Serpent. The Fearful Monks. The monstrous specters risen from the past, from her tormented childhood. The painful jumbled fragments of her memory. *They must have come from some other fortress; could they be here by chance?*

She counted the quarrels in her arrow-case. There were enough to kill the whole hooded lot of them, this whole venomous ensorcelment. But would she have time to load her weapon fast enough? She doubted that. She had the advantage of speed over the monks since she was mounted while the monks, at least in appearances, had come afoot. But alas, they blocked her way out, the narrow and single road which led beyond the rocky escarpment. *You see, death, death, death, it comes!* the birds cried in their cynicism. One of the monks lifted his hand, a bony, pale hand, which added a ghostly touch to the scene, theatrical as one could wish—and he spoke. *"You have nothing to fear from us, Lsi!"*

How do they know my name? After all this time and all the confused things between?

The hand traced abstract figures against the gray heavens. *We know that you were once kidnapped and that you have undergone terrible privations, that you have fallen under the spell of these cursed creatures. We have come very far to help you.*

(*No,* she told herself, *I have gone mad, or perhaps I'm dreaming, I glide and drift somewhere in another time, a time when—*)

While their companion spoke as if to hypnotize Lsi the other monks had begun to move in encirclement. Viciously they began to spread out. Under their open robes there were visible the metallic flash of sabers and daggers. The monks of the Great Serpent! Lis, suddenly chilled, was shaking from head to foot when her horse struck his shoe on a rattling rock. The noise shook her from the spell—alas, too late. They were quite close now. Almost touching her. In a desperate attempt to run she let off a shot, sighting on the monk who seemed to threaten her most immediately. Ssstk! The projectile made an ugly sound as it passed through the monk's chest. The zealot of the Great Serpent gave a mournful cry, then a horrid gargling sound before he dropped in a heap. Killed outright. The bolt had split his heart. Before she had the time to reach a second quarrel a strong hand grabbed her by the left boot, arms encircled her waist, disarming her with a humiliating ease which drew from her insults and outcries. *You have nothing to fear, Lsi. Even if, in your madness, you have killed one of us.*

Nothing to fear, nothing to fear—

Cried the birds.

With all her might Lsi thought of Bearface. Sped to him like a bolt from the arbalest, the message of her distress and her fear: *Help me— against the fangs of the Great Serpent!*

The roar was dreadful. It rushed into Lsi's ears, it walked in the gates of her comatose half-sleep. Perhaps it was the cacophony of the demon-realm.

But it was not—for—

Came the cold. A biting cold, which roughed her skin, ravished her flesh—the cold of storm. She opened her eyes and saw that she was naked and imprisoned in what must be a cavern near the sea.

The five surviving monks were there; they surrounded her, their hoods flung back, their eyes full of threatening glitterings. She wondered what they had done with the body of the one she had dispatched with the arbalest shot. She was stretched on the rocky ground, her arms and legs spreadeagled, wrists and ankles bound by thin leather thongs to heavy stone blocks. She belonged to them. They could do what they wished with her.

He who was the chief of the monks addressed her. "We are going to have to put you to the question, young woman. We do not shrink at anything we must do to get what we wish. You know that. We repent in advance of the torments and the humiliations we will be compelled to inflict if you are reticent. But we are persuaded that the light will return to your soul even before your flesh has been put to the test. We have observed what is going on in this region and we would like to know what is the significance of these movements and these—"

These men were nothing but spies. They doubtless preceded some numerous army whose purpose was— She tried not to think of that threat which her instinct told her was terrible, doubtless unavoidable. If they were spies, if they had the intention to draw from her by torture some military intelligence, she must hold out until they killed her, whatever was the issue of the question.

"You're a beautiful girl," said the chief of the monks in a detached tone. "It would truly be a pity to destroy your beauty."

She shut her eyes. She saw shining lightnings burst above a vast shadowy plain covered with an immense army on the march, infantry and cavalry.

They came to kill. To seal a painful old wound with the blood of other wounds; they came to sow the whirlwind; to make death spring from the earth like mushrooms after rain. They came to kill.

It was in the order of things, such as the Great Serpent knew them. Obscurely she had always known that the phantoms would ensnare her again. They would find her again, Shai and her, at the other end of the earth.

Dead men ride faster than the wind, faster than the wind—

The monk who commanded the brothers leaned forward, knelt near Lsi. His eyes were like two burning coals. In his right hand he held a dagger with a large curved blade.

"Listen," said the hooded monk. "Listen to this thunderous voice. It's the voice of the sea. I will tell you that your companion, this oath-breaker named Shai, has been taken by the pirates. I know too that the general of the Barbarians is beside himself. As if he had lost the son born of his own loins, the son that the gods had once refused to give him. I know all that, and many other things as well."

The dagger descended toward Lsi's belly. But a few centimeters from her navel it stopped, like a metal wasp retracting its sting.

"I can," said the monk, his gleaming eyes fixed on Lsi's belly, "destroy you slowly, I can gut you without killing you, dismember you slowly, drive you to madness with the sight of your own body cut apart bit by bit, my girl. And not release you till the last moment, when you will be no more than the least shred of life. But I am sure that your repentence is true, that you have it in your heart to return to your own kind. To bow before our Guide and our Master, the Great Regatherer of Lifeforce—"

You lie! You will not let me survive this interrogation. When you know what you want to know, you will bury your dagger in my heart or leave me here instead, in this damned cave. I shall be eaten alive by the crabs—

The curved dagger crossed those few centimeters and rested gently on Lsi's skin, three fingerwidths below the navel. The touch of the metal made her shiver. *Please, Bearface, you can't be far away— Can't my cry reach you, guide you to me?*

The monks had knelt and began to sing together a strange sequence of invocations. The effect of this odd dissonance was terrifying, destroying; it literally stripped the nerves; all the body went rigid; the muscles knotted; the guts spasmed; bones cracked; there was the need to scream but the throat was too painfully constricted.

The point of the knife pierced Lsi's skin. The pain was scant but the psychological effect produced by this brusque intrusion showed itself quite effective: the young woman felt that the dagger was plunged into her groin to the hilt. The monks raised the pitch, one of them pushing his voice into the upper registers so that she felt she must crack like a stem of glass.

With a maddening leisure the torturer-monk traced around Lsi's navel a little bloody line which soon took the form of a circle, or a snake which bit is own tail. Red serpent of destiny. The monk which sang the high harmony screeched now like a hysterical girl.

Lsi had lost no more than a few drops of blood but already panic was on her: a black and vicious bird which pecked away at heart and brain.

"You see," said the inquisitioner-monk, "I trace upon you the symbol of all-powerful wisdom. When you die, soiled or purified, your soul all trembling and bloodstained will tear itself from your belly to climb toward the abode of the dead. In spite of your crimes and your faults, your prayers will find an attentive ear."

Lsi's mouth opened and made a kind of uncontrollable spasm. *I want to speak; I want to tell them—*

"Don't struggle so. I haven't done anything

to you yet. Wait till I start to work on you in earnest."

The other monks sank now in a new harmony. Sweet as rotting fruit.

"As a beginning," the torturer-monk said gently, "I shall proceed to the removal of your right breast. Then—"

What can I do to make myself faint? To not feel anything? To escape this foulness?

Lsi gathered all her strength for one word. *"Wait!"*

The monk leaned forward as if he were about to kiss Lsi upon the lips. "You said something?"

Yes, I said wait. You can't do this to me. Cut me up alive. I want to answer your questions—

"You say nothing. I thought— Well, well, I shall start my work. Don't move now; you don't want to aggravate matters."

No. She contracted her muscles which were hard as those of a young amazon. She gathered all her strength, felt the cords holding her wrists, the blood running on her hands. The knife point slowly approached her right breast. The monk took his time; his eyes shone, filled with bile, and the fever in them mingled with anticipatory pleasure. *Maybe he really doesn't want to know anything at all. Maybe it's all a cruel game, an ugly sport—* At the moment when she was about to give way, drenched with oily sweat, bathed in it, her throat full of bitter vomit, the thongs which painfully held her right wrist slipped. She thought at first she had dreamed it in her mad lust to survive, to escape this hellish game. But a new effort told her that her right hand was going to be free of bonds in a very brief moment. The instinct of self-preservation acted for Lsi; necessity took the place of wit. She dug her nails into those gleaming eyes, fiercely, with all the strength she was capable of. The monk howled, brought his hands to his face, stupidly let go his dagger. The other monks interrupted their chant. Too shocked still to react. The dagger went to the hilt in the torturer's stomach; he rolled onto Lsi with a groan like a poled ox. But the young woman rolled him at once onto his side and with a sudden jerk recovered the dagger from the torn belly. A flood of blood gushed out and drenched Lsi's chest and face even as she attacked the thong that still held her left wrist.

"Whore!" cried the monk with the screeching voice. "Demon whore! You've killed two of us!"

All four of them had gained their feet. A burning hate was in the looks they aimed at the young woman. Hate and frustration. And they all four burst into voice. "Kill, kill the whore!"

*　.　*　　*

Talk or I'll kill you!

Calm down, hetman, said Kjul, his hand placed brotherlike upon Bearface's arm.

He was going to shout—*Your love for Shai misleads you*—but he restrained himself, for Kjul had no desire to fling oil on the hetman's rage.

Talk or I'll kill you!

The shaman under interrogation lifted his head, his throat caught in the noose. Bearface's huge fingers held firmly the leathern collar and the deadly wooden bar. *I'm going to squeeze him a little more.* The shaman writhed vinelike. The narrowing of the painful collar left him only the extremity of his breath. Fear darkened his eyes. *The boy is gone, the pirates took him, and what's more, you fucking bastard, the girl hasn't come back from her trek—*

Hetman, Kjul pleaded, *you can't sink to the level of these dogs! Don't soil yourself with killing them! We're the men of the plain and the forest, our destiny is written in the stars, in the sudden rising of the wind, in the winter ice, in the mist of our horses' breath— Our destiny is written in—*

I don't want to hear the voice of the tribe today—I want to strangle this dog! He wanted to strangle the dog and he pressed his throat to the last, wrung at his vertebrae—and suddenly he heard, still distant but coming like a thunder-roll, Lsi's voice, begging. *Help me—against the fangs of the Great Serpent!*

—"Kill, kill, kill, kill the whore!"

Their voices rasped while Lsi's mute cry pierced the cavern walls. It turned like a wing-shot bird, hurled itself up to the steepness of the cliffs, carried on the wind.

KAAAA   KAAAAA
KAAAA   KAAA-KILL-KILL-KILL

The bird died. It cried and died in the ice, against the sheer cliff. But it relayed Lsi's anguish across space. (And casting from him the grimacing shaman's face, Bearface cried: Keep him alive till I get back!)

Kill, kill—

They urged each other on but this blood-covered amazon, this young statue of wrath, daunted them. In so little time she had killed two of their number. Before they had even reached her she had cut the bonds which held her ankles and gotten to her feet, her breasts and her belly spotted with blood, long red trails running to her groin.

"Kill the whore!"

"Come ahead," Lsi shouted, "but hurry up about it!" She brandished her dagger and laughed nervously. If she had begun to howl like a she-wolf, the monks of the Great Serpent would not have been overwhelmingly surprised.

But this grace did not last. They wanted to get this over with. To destroy this young female who insulted them, who challenged them with flamboyant impudence. They parted the skirts of their habits and drew their curved-bladed sabers, dangerous weapons which could split a skull, cleave limbs with childish ease.

Lsi had only postponed the fatal moment. She would die anyway, but she would die quickly, without suffering, her head split by a saberstroke. That was better than seeing herself go on an ocean of pain, dismembered like a side of meat in the market while she was still alive.

The monks came closer, whirling their sabers. Their eyes now were cold and decided. Their anger seemed to have vanished entirely and their hate shone with a fierce spark in their slitted eyes.

Slowly, step by step, Lsi retreated toward a rocky slope. The sea thundered on. It seemed mindfully to underline the diverse phases of the combat.

One of the curved blades passed quite near Lsi. She thought she felt the breath of it on her throat. *Bearface, it's too late now. My voice hasn't reached you—* Lsi's heart was full of bitterness and wrath.

"Ha!"

One of the monks gave a high-pitched shriek; it was he who had screeched that incomprehensible invective. His saber, deftly handled, grazed Lsi's shoulder and brought a splash of blood. The pain did not come at once but the surprise paralyzed the young woman, opening her to the attacks of the sinister monks.

"Kill, kill, kill the whore!"

Four curved blades began their deadly rush.

In a last convulsion of vital force, Lsi hurled herself from the height of the rocks into the icy water which churned in the shadow of the sea cave.

The icy wave closed over the young woman like the maw of a ravenous beast, armed with a hundred thousand pitiless sharp teeth. In spite of the cold and the fear, she could hear far overhead the spiteful howls of the monks of the Great Serpent. Retreating a little—*To what death have I fled?* she thought. It was a twisted and cold little question, to which her wits did not know what to answer.

She had cast herself into the icy current for fear of the curved blades, to escape the most immediate danger. But like the most of her companions she was a very poor swimmer. For a moment she thought of ridding herself of her dagger, to be more free in her movements, then she thought that if some danger tracked her in the water, she was better off having a weapon to defend herself. It was a stupid thought, surely, but she clung to it like a drowning woman to a log.

She regained the surface and saw, standing on the rock, nimbused in a kind of spectral glow, the four yelling monks.

They waved their weapons at her and kept up their invective.

The cold was awful. It clasped her now in its great flaccid hands, put its thousand liquid mouths to her flesh.

Her ill luck had drawn back but a step or two. In a few moments her limbs would grow leaden, she would drift in a deadly loss of direction. She would die then, but with the bitter satisfaction of having cheated the monks of the spectacle of her ruin, of her slow and painful death. They could keep their base hunger. She set the knife between her teeth and began to swim toward the exit of the grotto. The crash of the waves had become deafening; they plunged into the cave in a kind of mindful wrath.

Something hissed wasplike near her ear. She realized that the monks were shooting at her with her own arbalest.

The push of the water became formidable and she was cast back the moment she tried to fight her way up the narrow channel which led to the sea. From outside she could hear the whistling of the wind.

Between her clenched jaws she still held the curve-bladed dagger.

She turned her head to see what the torturers were up to; they had vanished. All four of them.

The roar of the sea and the wind grew even louder, but suddenly it seemed to her that the elements were talking to her, encouraging her to persevere. A voice echoed in her head, warm and reassuring. *You have to keep your courage*, it said. *Lsi, you have to keep your courage.* Her arms grew heavier and heavier, and the cold clenched her belly and her chest in a painful constriction. But she held on because of that *voice* which was in her, suddenly—

Outside!

With that voice in her, which utterly possessed her, which screamed at her from the midst of her skull, to survive.

And she did survive. At the very moment when she might have given herself up to the violence of the sea, to its repeated battering, to the cold, she found herself outside—in the open air, with the wind and the salt and the cry of the birds. Fighting with renewed forces to get entirely clear of the channel of watery turbulence. A furious backsurge drove her onto a flat rock, partly covered her with grassy weed.

She clung there, her eyes stung with the salt, her jaws still clenched on the blade of the curved dagger. Slowly, her teeth biting the metal as if to draw its hard essence into herself, Lsi drew herself up onto the rock in a sort of obscene slither, as if the rock were a lustful beast with insatiable appetite. Her breast and belly slid on the bubbling, clinging tendrils of blue weeds. The touch of the weeds filled her with horror, but she knew that she had to overcome these flinchings of body and soul, to silence the cries of panic which came welling up from her subconscious.

Soon she was on her feet, standing on the rock, strange naked statue, her hair plastered down with salt water, her curved dagger in her hand. She had escaped the monks' sabers, but she was not safe yet. The surviving monks could not let her walk out from their hands and have her go alert the enemy camp.

She told herself that she was visible from a distance, standing on her moss-slick rock, and that she presented an ideal target for any moderately gifted archer. But she loathed the idea of lying down on that cold, mucky stone; she preferred to stay on her feet, at the risk of receiving full in the chest the brutal shock of an arbalest quarrel.

Her teeth chattered in the cold now so that

she could not close her jaws on the icy dagger blade.

"If they come," she said aloud, thinking of the hateful monks who had promised her the most awful torments, "I'll kill myself with the dagger. If I have the courage left, the strength—"

The sun went gold suddenly in the gray sky, like a vast flower spreading in a great autumn prairie. But it did not send any heat across space; it was cold, like a dead star. Finally her strength left her and she had to sit down on the blue-weeded rock, let the huge slimy mouth touch her intimately with its soft, cold caresses.

Time passed. As in a dream, she saw a veil drift into the fog of her thoughts, a triangular sail, like a shark's fin.

Parenthesis IV

NEW EPISODES IN THE CRYSTAL WAR

ONE: The world is the prey of the fires. The crystal bombs are like meteors which light this last night of the war. The combatants in their shining armor flee desperately in the false daylight of combat. Cries echo which no one can hear in the crash of crystalline explosions. The officers insult in vain their deserting companies, and their whips crack fire uselessly above the bloody-eyed deserters: there is no longer either victor or vaniquished, now that the great geological agony falls from the faded, broken skies.

Sun-fang is the prey of the flames. . . .

The crystal bombs rain down like shooting stars. . . .

TWO: The heat is harsh and consuming; one might think oneself prisoned in a metal egg heated to white heat. The convoy behind its dying locomotive drags itself toward the petrified dunes which edge the northern zone of the desert. The travelers have opened the windows, but there is not a breath of wind, and the sweat evaporated instantly on their cracked skins. Struggling, the machine feels as if it is walking over rails swollen by the sun's heat.

Brutal phantasm, a squad of hairy riders gallops before it, outside the subtle anvil of the light; later, during a brief flicker of time, the spectral Hunters ride even with the wheezing engine.

THREE: This world, said the man-with-eyes-like-coals, is Sun-fang in the language of necromants and the emperors of the Crystal City. But no one knows the origin of this strange name. There once existed on this planet whose two moons shine like daystars, powerful nations and shadowy powers, queens mad with self-love and magicians whose minds were gnawed by the acids of anguish.

But now the world belongs to the powers of sleep and night. The only rulers *here* are the invincible time-hunters who wander the Red Plain where the rails slowly rust, covered by knife-edged grass.

VI

THE CRYSTAL LEPER

Behind the crystal mask Captain Otman's voice formed his sentences with a dreadful regularity.

"You others," he said, "you people of the fortresses, have lived outside time, inside truth. While you raised the walls of your citadels, your high towers of guard and your formidable secret knowledge against the outside world, the outside world itself kept on living and dying, consuming and regenerating. Then came the Barbarians, who represented the raw, brutal force of the planet. They were the key that opened that dark doorway. Tools, perhaps, in a very complex game the rules of which elude even the players. An old story, you know. Very old, but most people never tire of it. For example those who, no matter when, no matter where, want power. The earth, you see, has become again a melting-pot of anarchy, at least in appearances, from which anything might come, a better world as well as worse. You fought at the side of the barbarians, for you had become one of their own. But this combat was of course only a phase. Then, obedient to some obscure call, the horde, or part of the horde, came to the shores of this redoubtable sea, this sea controlled by pirates whom you may just have escaped. That is the supposition that I make. You surely wonder too how we know all this about you. By what miracle, by what subterfuge? By what felonious act?"

Shai wanted to say something to stop even briefly this flood of words but a gesture of the silk-gloved hand imposed silence on him.

"No, don't seek to interrupt me." The crystal mask glittered in the sun. "There are so many things yet to say, which you have to know and think on.

"Over the years, or rather decades, men have evolved. The survivors of the crystal holocausts sometimes formed into desperate bands to wander the surface of a disfigured planet, while others, half dead, suffered strange mutations. Certain ones had acquired strange sensory powers, and slowly but surely they took it into their heads to create a new civilization.

"Yes, that's true, the evil had at least some fortunate outcome. Some of those who had been marked with what we call the crystal leprosy were transformed to become the new mankind. As if the horror held within itself its own cure. Must I tell you that I am one of these new men, and that—"

Could it be, Shai wondered with a sudden anxiety, *that this mask he wears is really his face?*

"I guess the questions you're asking, Shai. No, don't worry. I do have a face and this mask is only a symbol. It's just part of the etiquette. In the eyes of the pirates of the Archipelago I do have to keep up appearances."

How could one trust a man who hides his face behind a mask? I don't know what to think. I don't know what to believe. All my certitudes have fallen one after the other. All of them expect me to betray someone. What shall I do not to go mad in this mess? What is at stake in this mysterious war which engaged all these enigmatic organizations? Is there truly a war or one vast and subtle game? Who directs the world? The new masters—would they be better than the old? Would they not also unleash great conflicts, even genocides? What strange perversities hide behind this crystal mask? The plump shadow of Dr. Denner Pfeil returned to haunt Shai's thoughts. Ridiculous and monstrous

puppetmaster. The young man was persuaded
that he had a role to play in this mournful (?)
intrigue. And Syria? What value now had the
strange revelations that she had made to him,
yonder, in the Isle of the Swamps, Locus
Draconis, the Place of the Dragon? Sometimes
Dr. Pfeil appeared to him as a dear fat uncle,
sometimes to the contrary he seemed like some
sort of frightful old man with nasty, violently
ambitious intentions. How could one trust these
phantoms that rose out of the Earth's morbid
past?

"I can read in you," declared Captain Otman,
"that you doubt what I say. You think I only
intend to deceive you? Your hopes turn you
constantly toward your hetman, Bearface? But
was he not the first to deceive you? The fall of
the fortress of the Great Serpent ought to have
marked the dawn of a new era. But, remember,
Shai, this victory was quickly transformed to
defeat. You ran cold and long roads, and burning and dusty ones—and to do what when you
returned? Why, your war had only begun,
why—"

"I want to see your face!" Shai cried. "If you
have one which really is your own—"

Otman rose. In his hand suddenly shone a
metal object. "No one talks to me that way."

All his pleasantness, all his tolerance were
gone, had flown like mist in the sun. The shin-

ing object was trained on the young man's breast.

"You don't impress me," Shai yelled. "You talk, you talk, you play a role, and you prate endlessly about gods and the world, and—"

The wind billowed the silken robe, pressed upon it the motion of a veil spread against the winter sun, and the crystal mask exploded in rainbow darts. The object aimed at Shai's chest gave out a long sonorous vibration and the young man felt himself enveloped in a painful shudder, an electric caress writhing cruelly through his whole nervous system. His jaws clenched and his voice died on his lips. He fell in a heap among the rocks, the suffering set into his body like a venomed insect bite. He earnestly wished to lose consciousness, but the pain stayed alive and his mind stayed fearfully aware. His eyes plunged deep into the eyes of the crystal mask while the whole world consumed itself in the burning embrace of a giant sun.

"I am also the master of pain," said Captain Otman. "We are all the students of pain. You ought to know that."

Suddenly there were other men around the captain, men robed in silk and metal and whose masked faces had the terrible stigmata of the crystalline leprosy.

*   *   *

Dmitri Vashar contemplated with satisfaction
the high ramparts of the citadel of Orghedda.
He had had his army march as one man, without hearing the recriminations of his officers
or the indignant murmurings which rose occa-
sionally from the ranks of the mercenaries.
Aye, he had had his army march as a single
man. He, Lord Dmitri Vashar, tetrarch of night,
Holy Knight, Grand Liegeman of the Great
Serpent, Knight of the Right Hand, Guardian
of the Tradition and Familiar of the Temple.

And now the walls of the citadel of Orghedda
shone in the pale winter sun, the oriflammes
spread upon the wind.

"Lord," said a dark voice, "we are at the foot
of our task."

But Dmitri Vashar did not deign to respond
to the somber figure. He warmed his hatred in
the flames of his wrath. All this journey and
all this cold had not calmed his soul. Ice crys-
tals glittered on his violet cloak but his brow
shone with sweat and with fever.

"Orghedda, at last."

On the ramparts the trumpets sounded.

Orghedda! Last council before the tidal wave
of vengeance.

At Jermyn they had fallen on a band of
nomads, perhaps the hetman's spies. They had
captured them without exception and burned

them alive until there was nothing left of their carcasses but ash, which scattered on the wind. A happy omen—perhaps.

It was indeed a sailboat. A little craft with a mast and sail. Triangular as the sailfin of some great fish. The fishermen used such boats.

A wild hope stifled her breath. The chill which had gotten into her belly gave way to a strange flood of warmth when she sprang to her feet on that slimy rock, to signal her saviors. She waved her arms above her head and the dagger struck flashes from the wintry sun like a strange sickle. Cries and voices answered her appeals and she realized her mistake. The monks were sailing toward the rock.

Flee? The sheer cliff loomed over her. And in the time to reach the shore yonder even if her strength did not fail her halfway, she would have twice over been taken up by those monks who lusted for murder and revenge. A bird skimmed the dim green and gray shore and Lsi envied it as it sported there, its power to pass from one element to the other to escape any chance pursuers.

Driven on the wind, the little craft drew rapidly closer to the rock and the young woman could hear clearly the insults the monks hurled at her. *This time,* she thought, *I will not escape them. They have dead to avenge, instincts to satisfy. Surprise won't be on my side any longer.*

"You won't get me alive," she said. "I'll kill myself with my own hands before I serve as your sport."

The bark, carried by its triangular sail, was no more than a few cable-lengths from the rock. She had to decide, to gather up her courage. Bitter tears trickled down the young woman's face. She set the point of the knife under her left breast, remembering the ugly purpose of the monk she had stabbed. They had won the hand, whatever she did and whatever she tried now. They were evil and despair personified.

Shaken by long tremors of terror and cold, she cast a last look at the boat and its four occupants. The monks were maneuvering boldly, pushing the little sailboat among the reefs. Two of the monks brandished long hooks with which they might draw the boat into range of the rock when the moment should come to get to action.

"You think you can play games with us, whore!"

Oh, if the wind would turn; if it should drive their boat on a rock, if they all should die? That's stupid; the wind won't turn, and I'm the one who's going to die.

She pushed gently at the knife and the point

gouged a millimeter or two inward, drawing a small runnel of blood. The pain as well as the effort appalled her. *I shall never have the courage,* she thought. *Never.*

She shut her eyes to concentrate, to gather all her will. There was a strident cry and she suddenly interrupted the fatal effort of her right hand. The triangular sail was afire, wing of fire in a gray sky, while one of the monks was leaning overboard as if he had been vomiting. When he rolled into the water she realized that something had happened which was going to turn the situation around. With a hoarse cry she turned toward the shore: in the hollow of the cliff, in that place where the waves came to beat themselves at the rocky shore, Bearface and Kjul had brought the monks' boat under the fire of their laser.

Lsi clenched her teeth, youthful fury returned from a long journey, lately escaped from hell. "You will know the anger of the Bear," she shouted. "You're nothing but stinking rats, and the Bear's jaws will break your backs! Far too good a death considering what you offered me!"

The three surviving monks had thrown themselves down on their bellies on the bottom of the boat, which was now traveling at the whim of current and wind. With a frightful crack the little craft came to break against Lsi's rock. Two of the monks were swept away by the waves, turning and wailing in the backsurge, trying in vain to crawl up onto the reef on which the young woman had taken refuge. Their fright-glazed eyes saw the naked amazon hurl herself on them and slash their clutching hands with dagger strokes until the blood spurted out, mixing itself with sea-salt. They loosed their grips and wailed in impotent hatred before the waves strangled their plaints and they vanished into the darkness.

Panting, Lsi let herself collapse onto the rock without so much as noticing the repulsive touch of the blue weed. She was safe and whole and that was the only thing that mattered. Safe and whole after all these hours of misery . . . She had a moment of dizziness and shut her eyes to blot out the sight, to let the exquisite music of the sea revive her, carry her into its primordial rhythm.

But a voice she well recognized now burst into her skull. *Watch out!*

Her lids lifted with the rapidity of instinct. She had counted wrong: there was a survivor. He stood over her and his bloodied face seemed twisted by some hideous malady. In reality his features were convulsed in a fierce, unspeakable hatred. In both hands he had the hilt of his curved dagger, like the high priest of some bloody religion or a sea demon suddenly risen from the waves. "I'll get you after all!" cried the madman and folding at the knees he cast himself at his victim.

Lsi was unable to avoid it, to roll backward to put herself out of reach of that mortal blow. Ha!

The monk lost his balance when the young woman's knee, flying wild in a panicked spasm, took him in the belly. He swore, which was improper for a monk, cursing the gods briefly, and he sprawled at full length on Lsi's panting body. The dagger blade had buried itself in the shoulder of the beaten amazon. Lsi cried out, certain she was wounded to the death, and her cry mixed with a dreadful gurgling coming from the twisted, grimacing mouth of the zealot of the Great Serpent. A flood of black blood poured over Lsi's face, and she realized that in falling on her the killer had impaled himself on the dagger her hands still held clenched in the biting cold, its point aloft. *What does it matter?* she thought. *I'm dying with him.* The flood of blood covered her, strangled her, filled her mouth, expanded within her like a red salt hydra. An odious mockery of a kiss. A broken mannequin, grotesque, the monk moved against her, shaken in the final spasm of his death agony. *I die violated by a corpse!* she thought with a mournful chuckle. *These thoughts are ridiculous. I am already dead.*

* * *

Shai wakened in a close space, made of metal. It reminded him at once of the strange chambers of Locus Draconis, the Dragon's lair. And of Dr. Denner Pfeil.

"That's all," he said aloud. "There has to be sense to all of this. Or I shall go mad."

"Oh yes," said a gentle voice that came from a sort of oval light set in the center of the platform, "all of this is perfectly logical."

"Who are you?" asked Shai.

There came a clear laugh, which seemed faintly familiar to the young man. "I am Dunja IV, grand duchess of Carniole. But you'll see me in a moment."

"Can I please know where I am?"

"You're in a ship. A modern ship, and not one of these primitive craft the pirates of the Archipelago use. Logically you ought to ask me now the next question: Where are you taking me?"

"I'm not crazy. You surely wouldn't answer that question."

"You think yourself quite intelligent. Perhaps you really are. Go be a nice fellow and sit down, Shai; and wait for me. I won't be long."

The voice contained an edge of mockery. But not the least malice.

Shai shrugged and went to sit on a chair that looked rather stark but which comfortably settled itself to the lines of his body. He stayed watchful, fearing to let himself be won over by this temporary and certainly deceptive sense of wellbeing. A door which he had not noticed until then opened in the wall, affording passage to the grand-duchess Dunja and her magnificence. She was a grand and majestic woman, well suited to bear the sonorous title which was hers, of a middle age but still handsome, accustomed to be attended, listened to, served with zeal. Her dark eyes shone with a quite youthful ardor and her hair—even if it was streaked with gray, had lost none of its curl or luster.

If for no other reason than to tell her that he was not happy with the way they treated him, Shai would have wished to stay seated in apparent indifference, meeting the newcomer with a hostile attitude, but this strange lady commanded respect. He perceived from her an aura of power and authority, such a magnetism that he got up in spite of himself and bowed deeply.

"Don't stand on formalities," said the grand duchess. "My title is only a disguise, like everything else in this world since the Forces of Chaos and Night have run wild across seas and lands. What disguise do you wear, Shai? To bring you here, to this ship, we had to use trickery, and finally force. Now the strings are almost all tied—in so far as things concern you. So my work will be finished on this part of the planet and I will be able to go back to my own lands."

They sat down in chairs which stood paired.

"I hear nothing but people who talk to me in riddles," Shai said. "Since I was captured by the pirates, my lady, I have been passed from hand to hand, I've been humiliated, cheated—"

"I understand your impatience and your indignation, but the reality is not as complicated as you might think. It is only confounded by the disorders of history. By long years of war and lies. Captain Otman tried to explain a few episodes of our past but you were overwrought; you wanted to solve the problem your own way, a little like the young king of Macedon who sought the solution of his riddles with the edge of his sword."

Shai stirred nervously in his chair. Dunja's hand rested on his shoulder as if to convince him to stay calm and reasonable.

"Civilization, since the crystal wars ravaged the world, has passed through incarnations which are often grotesque, lived through sad and deceptive metamorphoses. But good, you see, has finally come from the chrysalis of evil. We others who retain some fragments of the ancient knowledge, have made alliance between past and future. There's an old paradox to the effect that those who think they govern are only puppets . . . survivors of an era of revolution . . . perverted symbols. . . ."

"You mean the people of the fortresses? The servants of the Great Serpent?"

"Yes, of course, but the pirates too, these parasites of baroque and bloody philosophy. And there are still others. The inhabitants of the celestial Dragon, with their powerlessness and their regrets—but they will destroy themselves without any outside help. It's only a question of time; their sterility seems definitely without remedy."

"And what am I to do in this long history?"

"Your place is all marked out, Shai. You chose your side from the time you delivered the fortress into the hands of the Horde. And you chose the right side. Our role, my friend, is an important but secondary role, and we only rarely appear on stage."

Anguish returned to the young man's heart. Dunja's words, far from reassuring him, plunged him into increasing disarray. The idea of playing any great part in the theater of the world inspired him with nothing but fear and distaste. Since the day he had learned to think for himself, he had found nothing but lies, plotting, treason. Life was nothing but a long wandering across the devastated territories of his conscience.

"There are men stronger and more intelligent than I," said Shai. "I don't want to carry a load like that on my back." He thought of Bearface, of his formidable power over men and his great wisdom. He closed his eyes and a vision suddenly crossed his mind: the hetman galloped alone across a desert waste, all white with snow, and ice and blowing mist. He was riding against the wind, and the edges of his thick cloak rattled like standards. Soon he disappeared into the white ocean, dissolved, diluted, a ghost which no longer had form or shape. Then the land closed itself and the winter devoured everything.

". . . up to you to decide, of course," she explained precisely, she who called herself Dunja IV, grand duchess of Carniole, "but the moment will doubtless come when you will be ready to take your fate into your own hand."

Shai could not decide between anguish and relief. The things Dunja said encouraged him to believe that he had suffered under the venomous influence of the Captain-pasha and of Dr. Foskus, and that seemed to him a good reason to recover his courage now, but there had been this brief vision, this white imagery which had haunted his soul. Must he see in it some sort of omen, or a warning?

"Come," said the grand duchess, "let's go up to the bridge, for your voyage is already ending."

*　　*　　*

On the bridge of the strange ship there were neither mast nor sails, but Shai had read too many forbidden books when he was still the confidant of Dr. Magnus not to know it was a propeller which drove them. Captain Otman was there, still masked in crystal and robed in silk. In his gloved hands he held a long telescope.

Certain men of the crew, almost all marked with the crystal leprosy, were busy at mysterious tasks.

"I'm happy to say that our young friend is getting on very well in spite of the shock treatment I was obliged to inflict on him," said Captain Otman. "Impetuosity is youth's privilege. No one aboard this ship would dream of holding him accountable for his attitude."

Shai decided that the man in the crystal mask was offensive in talking about him like that in the third person. That held as much of outrage in it as it did of challenge. At least he was glad that there was to be no second trial of him, and it was thanks to that, that the captain made a point of testing his composure.

"Let be! Our young friend as you say, has certainly learned his lesson. He will know how to remember us, our concern and the regard we have for him."

"You're right as usual, Dunja; a few hours

can change a man more profoundly than ten years."

Shai surmised that behind the captain's emphasis was a purpose which went beyond the banalities of the conversation.

Yonder the coast was clearly discernible. He recognized the rocky strand and beyond that the cliff where the old man had established his last home. His heart beat strongly, as when one comes home from a very long voyage: the captain was right, for he had aged in these few dozen hours of captivity.

The grand duchess came to him and took him by the arm familiarly as if she had been an old friend or a distant relative. "We are observers. We do not intervene until it becomes *truly* necessary."

I have already heard someone hold forth such a theory. Far from this sea, but on an island just the same. Perhaps it was on that dragon's lair, in the middle of the swamps. Yes, it was that, the inhabitants of the island. The survivors of outer space, claiming they too could not interfere in the affairs of Terrans. Who talked of Good coming from the Chrysalis of Evil?

"You were born under a lucky star, young Shai," said Dunja IV. And she truly had the tone of a queen when she said that. Her lips shone with a brilliant flush and she looked much younger now. She went on. "I don't know if we shall see one another again, but that's not important."

Shai thought that he had now to speak words of recognition, words carefully chosen as those which had come from the lips of Dr. Magnus, to prove to the grand duchess that her kindness had not been wasted, that he was a cultured young man, full of resources which he knew he owed to her, who reigned over the land of Carniole. (Did such a place truly exist? Or was it only another jest, another avatar, a mask?) But he had difficulty framing his thought; he did not find the words he sought with such anxiousness.

"I want to say—" he began in a very ordinary way.

The grand duchess lifted a languid arm and made a gesture which meant: don't bother; I know what you're trying to tell me. All that is meaningless. Go back to your people and try to be watchful.

He realized that Dunja IV was really speaking to him, that she was giving him now all sorts of advice and suddenly he was irritated. He felt anger well up in him, for he was like a child that everyone in the world felt appointed to order or worse, advise.

Captain Otman showed him the coast which was quite close and of which he could now see the details. "We're going to let you off there, in that cove. Prepare to get into the skiff."

Several men of the crew drew near, silent and efficient, and Shai remarked once more on their faces the ravages of the crystal sickness. He shivered as if he feared even yet some trap would appear at the last moment, but the grand duchess leaned toward him tenderly and taking him by the shoulders as one bids farewell to a son whose loss one fears, she kissed him on the brow, almost furtively.

A little later, as the boat danced over the waves carrying him from the strange metal ship, he felt an intense, poignant emotion, which wrenched his heart. While the sailors labored, leaning silently on the oars, Shai realized that he had crossed a new threshold, that he had found himself in the path of new extravagances of destiny and that in all events the traces of recent experience had perished of the cold.

When the seamen let him off on the shore he tried to wave a last farewell to them, but their indifference made him understand that their worlds were two isles divided by the terrible seas of space and time.

VII
THE MASSACRE OF ZABAR

Lord Dmitri Vashar poured himself a new cup of wine. His throat was dry and burning, a gulf of fire. The wine flowed slowly down his throat and the great warrior who traveled with the wind of night stretched a leather-gloved hand toward the naked breast of the courtesan who had anointed her whole body with aromatic oil. In the high, leaping flames, the faces of the officers of the Tetrarch of Night seemed no more than brazen masks.

Crescendo.

Sublime crescendo.

Already the xopal poets were singing the praise of the triumphant general. He had beaten the babbling hordes who meant to put the world to torch and sword, and now in the great shadowed halls, the echoing passages of the fortress of Orghedda, Dmitri Vashar, Holy Knight, Grand Liegeman of the Great Serpent, Knight of the Right Hand, Guardian of the Tradition and Familiar of the Temple, soberly reflected upon his exploits.

The battle of Zabar.

For example—*Zabar*. A name which began to echo like a rallying cry, to convince the warriors of the citadels that their days were yet long, that their death was yet distant.

Sublime crescendo.

Sang the xopal poets:

Liege knight of the Right Hand
You have cut off one hundred thumbs
You have drawn a line of fire and blood
Dmitri Vashar
Tetrarch of Night
You roar like the Snow Tigers
We salute you, we worship you
Dmitri Vashar, You who know where wind
the ways of fate . . .

His hand dallying between the legs of the courtesan, Dmitri Vashar recalled the matter of the hundred thumbs.

It had been well before reaching the stage of Orghedda, in the outposts of the Tyrana Depression.

There had been a battle. A terrible battle.

When he had finally reached the winter quarters of the Horde. His cavalry, his infantry, his archers, his slingers, his riflemen had burst out into his countryside, wolves of fire, dogs of death.

Zabar!

Death drifted in the air like bloody orgasm.

Shai and Lsi were silent. A vast shadow spread its wings like a nightmare predator and settled between them. Incapable of speech, they had become victims of their memories. In a strange sense the young woman felt herself still stained as if the monk's blood spurting over her at the instant of his obscene death had hideously impregnated her. As for the young man, he could not keep his own memory from painting with dark delight the lecheries of Zaphyria and Aella.

They stayed that way, their eyes lost in nothingness, searching in the light of frail existence for the approach of night.

During this time, in his house, the hetman, surrounded by those closest to him, presided over a kind of war council. He had been glad to keep Shai out of it. The news that the young woman had given him did not cease to disturb him. He had wanted to know if the monks who had humiliated and insulted her were truly the spies of a formidable force or some scattered remnants of a company of bandits. His instinct told him that they were the forerunners of the powers of the night.

The Great Serpent had a persistent life.

It was preparing a heinous vengeance.

Shai and Lsi were silent. Their hands rested on their thighs like dead things, separate from them.

Dmitri Vashar was satisfied. He left behind him a veritable road of blood, a red scar which impressed upon the earth the might of his army, the curse of his name. *Let no one escape,* he had ordered, *no one tell what happened here!* Then he had changed his mind. He had cut off the thumbs of fifty surviving warriors and ordered them to take a message to Bearface. He had carried out the sentence himself, cutting off with blows of his axe the hundred thumbs of the fifty warriors. *Nothing like bloody examples,* he had confided to his captains who foreknew the value of surprise. *When these fifty messengers tell Bearface what had happened on the plain of Zabar, he cannot help but tell his people about it. He will have to confess that the part of the horde he left behind him no longer exists, that the women and the children have fallen into our hands, that the captives whom he had tried to win to his cause have now returned into the bosom of the great religion. He will know, and his people will know too, that he is cut about his roots, caught between two fires. And courage will surely desert his soldiers.*

And now, under the echoing vaults of the citadel of Orghedda, which no one had ever taken; which was like the venomous heart of the Great Serpent—in this immense hall where blazed tall white metal cressets, while whole trees were consumed in the monumental hearths, Dmitri Vashar tasted the pleasure of the imminence of his victory, the first fruits of his vengeance. His right hand, which he had finally ungloved with a kind of cruel languor, brutally caressed the young courtesan's belly.

As the reputation of the Guardian of the Tradition had preceded him within the walls of the fortress, the girl kept from demonstrating her displeasure. Fear had slipped deep inside her, and she wondered why this man who leaned above her with clenched teeth, with slitted eyes, had wanted her to share his couch. It seemed he had fallen asleep, and only the hand which played its cruel game between her legs, the meaning of which escaped her, proved that he was conscious of her existence. The xopal poets whose hoarse voices skillfully rendered all the nuances of epic song, persisted in their celebration of the exploits of the Tetrarch of Night.

Dmitri Vashar was far away in his red dream. He imagined the company with the severed thumbs arriving in the camp of his enemies, throwing dismay into the ranks of the barbarians. He portrayed to himself in manic detail their faces twisted with anguish; heard, as if he were there, the cries of the women and the wail of children, as the warriors held up their mutilated, useless hands.

The courtesan's groan drew him suddenly from his triumphant dream.

The grand duchess fretted somewhat. The image of the young man refused to leave her mind. *There is no chance,* said the philosophers of her country, *only destiny. Destiny plays with marked cards, but it finally wearies of its own game and it wants to throw down its power. That's what men call chance.*

Dunja IV, grand duchess of Carniole, grand actress of the Crystal Theater, lit a cigarette and drew in a long breath of smoke, inhaling to the depths of her soul. She was anxious to return to her fief, to the underground retreat she had built in the ruins of the town of Mahagonny. She was in haste to get back to familiar things, her monitor screens and her books.

When the effects of the drug began to make themselves felt, she wondered if Shai was still in the game, now that he was aware of a few of the pieces of the puzzle, or whether he would die in the great battle that was in the offing.

Slowly, regretfully, she slid into a liquid sleep.

The dreams which waited for her were not at all bright.

Captain Otman's ship traced a white wake in the sea. Its engines worked at full capacity. The coast had long since vanished.

Shai and Lsi lay side by side in the dark. The menacing shadow which had slid between them had finally disappeared, but there remained something of it crouched in the corners of the silence. The world tonight seemed strangely dead. Whatever one did, it remained haunted by leering, pitiless presences. Although their hands touched in the depths of the dark, the two lovers did not speak, did not find words capable of exorcising the demon silence. During a brief interlude of sleep Lsi had dreamed that she lay again on the slimy rock, alone and naked under a stormy sky. Her belly was swollen, and between her legs she felt an awful pressure. She thought that she was in labor, that the effort of her entrails was about to bear fruit. Desperately alone on her rock, surrounded by the crash of the waves, beslimed by the caress of the weeds, she pushed with all her might, her hands pressed to her deformed belly to expel the panting thing which was in her and which had been engendered by an obscene corpse. She came out of this dream screaming, her hands clutching her belly.

"The thing, the thing, the thing, it's clawing me, it's tearing me apart!"

A superstitious dread poured over Shai. It was all his fault, for he had blasphemed the Great Serpent and vastly confounded the established order. Betraying his own people, he had loosed a clockwork mechanism. Something, somewhere had started working, slowly, inexorably. And it was impossible to escape it.

When Lsi, trembling, had told him her dream, he suddenly found gestures to comfort her, words to console her; but later when they had made love, without really reaching that place which goes beyond pleasure, they fell silent again.

Stretched at Lsi's side, their hands clenched together, the young man had the vision of Dmitri Vashar on the ring-road of the fortress of the Great Serpent, his pitiless eyes and his immaculately gloved hands. And he heard him speak again. *I have to take you with me, one of these days. You'll see. When you leave my hands, you'll have nothing to fear from any man. Even the demons will flee your coming.*

But this night was cold; its heavy cloud hid the baleful moon; the young man feared demons less than he feared the immaculately gloved hands of Dmitri Vashar, those hands which could rise out of the dark at any moment and reduce to void his most intimate dreams, his most dearly held ambitions. Instinctively his hands came to embrace his young companion, hot and trembling in all this cold. They filled themselves with her presence, modeled her shape, suddenly eager to explore in that warm the proof of his own existence. *It's my fault,* he thought. *I'm to blame. Everything I touch I destroy, I turn to ashes. I shall go to Dmitri Vashar. I shall cast myself at his feet, I shall ask him the grace of liberty and life for Lsi, free passage for my companions. . . . I'm the one he wants.*

Lsi's hands came to the surface of the dark lake to surround Shai's body, to draw him from the depth of the warm, soft mud.

Lord Vashar, I beg you— Madness. A man would have to be mad to cast himself thus into the wolf's jaws. Why would Dmitri Vashar accord them any mercy when he had the whole world in his hands?

A whole gallery of faces paraded before his closed eyes. Dr. Foskus, the Captain-pasha, the admiral, Otman and his crystal mask, the grand duchess and her words— Adventurers and actors, brigands and philosophers. With all his heart he missed Dr. Magnus, the long evenings in the citadel library, in restlessness and excitement . . . Then, precise, cutting his dark thoughts with exactness, Bearface's sending settling into his mind: *Terrible things are on the wind. You need all the courage you have. It's important you look ahead. Not back. That's the way the wind blows. You know more things than I do. You believe that you're going mad. But no one goes mad that quickly. And especially not you.* Bearface's sending was a dagger in his mind.

Dmitri Vashar drew himself up to his full height in the great hall of the citadel of Orghedda. His arms lifted toward the shadowy vaults. "Get out, all of you," he cried. "Leave me alone!"

As the young courtesan sat up trembling he said dryly: "No. Not you. You, you stay with me."

The officers and the xopal poets, all the diners, all the sumptuously clad girls, left the hall.

The general remained alone with the courtesan in the great hall with its strange flickerings of light. In the subtle play of fire and torches the hands of the maddened conqueror shook like two irritable animals. With dismay the young woman remarked that the right hand of her lord and master was missing two fingers. This tardy discovery drew from her a mournful moan: this hand was the claw of a bird of prey, which could tear at her with a cruel carelessness. She did not know that Dmitri Vashar's right glove had been provided with a mechanical device that felt quite supple to any touch, letting a man as skilled as he and as combat-trained use the sword and axe. But in the citadels of the established Order, war was a men-only affair.

She drew herself aside, as if to make herself forgotten, fearing new brutality: in her eyes fear showed, but also fascination. The reputation which preceded Dmitri Vashar in all his movements had of course been gossiped in the gyneceum in Orghedda. Some of the women who claimed to be well-informed had talked of the virility of the Holy Knight with obscene superlatives. But to a woman they had deplored his coldness and his lack of consideration.

"Come here," Dmitri Vashar ordered, "don't stay there shaking in your corner."

The young woman approached him slowly. She looked like a little naked, fearful animal, hypnotized by the serpent. *In the hands of this man,* she thought, *my experience will do me no good: that man is spawn of the Dragon.*

"You wonder why I ordered you to stay with me? Don't you think I might be in an amorous mood? You think me brutal and cold. Maybe you even think, deep inside, that I am a demon." Dmitri Vashar's eyes were two icy opals. They shone, these cold and distant stones, like two dead stars in an eternal night; they swept the young woman to frozen lands where the simple thoughts of mortal beings had no value.

"I don't know if you can understand me," rasped the son of the Serpent, "and I don't expect much of you, poor whore, but I'm going to try to explain it to you."

The courtesan could not stop her limbs from shaking. Her teeth shocked together while her mind registered with horror the things her master said. They were words foretelling disgrace and death, heinous promises and threats. . . . "I can't keep all this rage inside, bitch!"

When he laid her on the pavings, she kept for the moment the illusion that he was going to act like all other men, for he entered her brutally while his implacable hands moved over her, bruised her with a growing wrath. But she realized that his manhood in her was cold, (as that of a demon, as that of a creature who wandered the icy wastes) enormous and painful. She dared not defend herself or cry aloud: if she looked as if she might oppose his will, would he not kill her to assuage his hate?

A moment earlier, Dmitri Vashar had been in the midst of triumph, listening not without complacency to the xopals vaunting his deeds, elaborating upon his cruelties. Now wrath and hate had overcome him, for suddenly he had remembered a time when he had lived in bright sunlight, when he had benefited from the protection and the glory of the Great Serpent. When the Bear's horsemen had not yet come from the forest. This blessed time, when everything was in its place, when masters were masters and slaves were slaves. This time was finished. Because of a tiny grain of sand in the works of the machine, he had been driven into the cold and the night; he had been constrained to leave his fief, in haste and without honor. He had become himself nocturnal and cold, regrouping under his command legions of shadows. And it was perhaps not without a certain irony that his allies had given him the resonant title of Tetrarch of Night.

In a moment of clarity, as if somewhere an invisible magician had let off a magnesium flash, Dmitri Vashar had seen the red and gaping wound of his honor.

Teeth clenched, eyes shining like the eyes of the Golden Serpent, he labored over the terrified courtesan, pouring into this inert body all the excess of his hatred. All the while knowing that no cruelty, no excess could pour balm on the seeping wound. Even when he had killed the Bear and the young dog with his own hand, he was not sure that he would recover his peace. The flames that had driven him from the fortress which the gods themselves had declared untakeable still burned high and clear. He would need oceans of blood to put them out, red tides, crimson cataracts to cover them at last, forever.

Dmitri Vashar's hands closed on the young courtesan's throat, unconsciously perhaps, and began to squeeze that tender flesh. The girl tried to struggle, to groan, to ask mercy, but the incubus whose cold filled her up with a suffering which slowly numbed her senses, had long since passed the borders of perception. He sent her sliding into death with a truly demonic skill.

When the fifty thumbless warriors entered Bearface's camp it was impossible to keep the matter quiet. The fifty warriors cried out their rage in the square, their eyes haggard, their bodies shaken with furious spasms. They held out their mutilated hands, crying out long curses. Now they said, now they were nothing, they could no longer be warriors; they could not handle axe or blade. It was forbidden them to think of vengeance. In their helplessness they told how they had crossed the vast wastes, skirted death, defenselessly escaped from countless dangers. They had come to warn Bearface of the sack and massacres that would not spare this region. They had come to tell what had happened yonder at Zabar. Words sometimes failed them to express the horror which continually shone in their eyes.

Without knowing it they sang the paean of Dmitri Vashar in their own way.

A mortal cold had fallen on the camp.

The hetman listened to these messengers of death chant their cruel praise. He wanted to ram their words down their throats, to erase with one axe-stroke these fear-ravaged faces, these grimacing masks which endlessly recited this absurd hymn to their own defeat.

His mind reviewed a fantastical spectacle: Metal regiments invaded the countryside. Their speed was considerable. They came in an infernal music, marshaled by demons with whips of fire. Burning everything in their path.

They advanced in the midst of a brutal music, but without uttering a word. And the hetman saw that the soldiers who composed this army were not truly human. They were invincible. A soulless multitude.

When he came back to himself, drunk with rage, the thumbless men still spoke as if in some trance.

Then the Bear began to growl. His powerful voice came up out of his gut. "You have survived a frightful time," he said, "a time blacker than night and more burning than hellfire, but why do you come to trouble our hearts? Have you taken oath to make us weak and trembling? We are all appalled by your tale, but our wrath is stronger than our dismay."

But the fifty warriors would not be calmed so quickly.

Their lips kept drooling words.

Their long voyage across solitude, fear, and cold had reduced their sanity to a small weak flame.

VIII
DMITRI VASHAR

The day was gray and cold. Clouds amassed on the indistinct line of the horizon, and on the mountain precipices famine-stricken beasts made known their sad laments.

The four riders who followed the bottom of the canyon, between two sheer walls, saw the horizon only as a thin gray slice, crushed beneath the weight of the clouds. A few hours before, they had left behind them the fortified camp, the warriors still asleep; and now cold surrounded them, dug its many needles into their flesh, rendered their gestures slow and heavy.

Shai, over Bearface's objections, had decided to join a group of scouts.

The three riders who accompanied him were experienced warriors, who had ridden through all the hazards of war, who knew all the subtle tricks of the trail. Their stolid silence set Shai ill at ease.

At the end of these hours of riding in this difficult terrain, he felt depressed, useless, even a hindrance. He had continually mulled over the events of these recent days, dissecting them, lining them up in his memory to the point of obsession.

He felt the inexorable approach of his old enemy. Every road, inevitably, led to him. On the frozen highways of this winter, Dmitri Vashar came bringing desolation and death.

The beasts which had lately been singing their sinister, depressing song were silent now, and their silence seemed more troubling than their hopeless lamentations.

Now that the meeting with his cruel adversary took on more and more the feeling of an inescapable event, Shai wondered why destiny had gone to such lengths to complicate his life, when his route could have been all marked out. When he could have become a squire to Dmitri Vashar and he might have followed him on the paths of glory, become in the hands of this byzantine but perhaps genial master a great strategist, a leader of men.

He shivered: He could not have become such a leader of men. In the gloved hands of Dmitri Vashar, in his fingers that mutilation had not made less powerful or less dangerous, he would have become no more than a poor stammering wreckage. The officer had surely detested him from the beginning, his warrior's instinct forewarning him that Shai was not an apprentice like other apprentices.

At the moment the little band reached the bottom of the valley, the rider in the lead lifted his hand in an imperious gesture, forcing his companions to halt. Still without saying a word, he pointed to the bottom of the valley, to the place where it, following the rivercourse, came out in the likeness of a road. This virtually unknown track climbed toward the heights of the canyon, a hidden observation point for the hetman's watchers. Dmitri Vashar must have at his disposal a wealth of spies and the resources with which to bargain with traitors as well as with mercenaries: At the edge of a leafless wood, evidently without fear of any possible attack, a squad of enemy riders had made their camp. From all evidence, Dmitri Vashar's troops had wasted no time. Very fortunately Shai's companions were no strangers to the wildlands, and their keen eyes were only rarely misled.

"How many of them are there?" asked Shai, his heart beating.

"Hard to say. More of them than us, anyhow."

"And what are we going to do?"

Pause.

"I count at least two dozen horses. If we engage them, we're dead."

A heavy silence followed Shai's somewhat redundant statement.

"Who's talking about engagement?" said Bekhr then, Bekhr, oldest of the three scouts. "You, huh?"

The words fell heavy on Shai's heart and against all effort to the contrary he felt himself desperately remote from these men for whom he felt such affection. Perhaps they thought he had become the hetman's prince, that he was no longer a man of their kind, brought up in their ways and their customs.

"I commend myself to your wisdom, Bekhr," Shai said, careful to keep things peaceful between himself and the old scout. "You do what you want, no question. What are we going to do?"

Bekhr shrugged. For a fleeting moment his eyes traced the swooping track of a bird in search of prey. Then: "We're going to go back, of course. These whoresons have to be part of Dmitri Vashar's advance guard, the thumb-cutter. I hope he keeps thinking he's unbeatable. That's how a man makes his dumbest mistakes."

In fascination, Shai kept staring at the bottom of the valley, the grove of naked trees, the horses of the enemy scouts.

Maybe they're not as dangerous as they say. Maybe Dmitri Vashar isn't as frightening as my boyhood memory of him. With a little luck, he'll be nothing but a bloody nothing, like so many others I've met in my travels—.

(Bearface had made a mistake in scattering his forces, in not taking the offensive. He ought to have sown the enemy general's route of advance with traps and ambushes. Instead, he had counted on the weakness of the inhabitants of the citadels, on their rivalries, their old dissensions. He had been wrong in following his dream of a just and prosperous world, where men of the plain and the forest could live in peace and security. He had been wrong. . . . Indeed, but his dream was that of an aging chief, whose thoughts were long and generous, who feared being ridden down by his death before he had been able to finish his work, before he had given his people a reason to hope for a future less dark, less chaotic. How could a man like him decide to pass such judgment on Bearface? Why, the hetman had taught him to live instead of cringing like a dog!)

There was a sudden movement. As if somewhere in the trail of Shai's vision a bright-feathered bird had abruptly taken flight. He gave a cry to warn his companions (which ordinarily would have been a great mistake) but Bekhr had already had wind of something and sent his horse shying.

Too late!

A sudden hail of arrows fell from the canyon walls, taking them unaware. Shai set spurs to his horse at the very instant a flight of arrows hit two paces away. They fell short: luckily for him, the enemy had fired short.

Without thinking, taken completely off guard by the suddenness of the attack, Bekhr's two scouts whirled their horses, having no desire to be killed. Since only the patrol leader and Shai were armed with blasters, and they were out in the open and presenting a clear target, they tried to flee the way they had come in.

The shouts of their attackers soon showed them that they had fallen into ambush. Before and behind, the rocks swarmed with enemies. Bekhr was the first to realize it.

"It's finished! There're at least fifty of them! We've fallen into it like raw recruits—"

It was the last thing he said. An arrow caught him in the left eye and pierced his brain. He was dead before he hit the ground. Shai and the two other scouts circled back to back in a deadly carousel, avoiding missiles as best they could.

Then the young man heard his companions cry out and knew that he was the only one left alive.

A crushing weight hit his neck and he lost consciousness.

Funereal, constant, the drums beat. Their rhythm never varied, and this monotony was very like a deathsong. They beat as they would have beat at the gates of hell, announcing the long parade of demons in ranks and in order of precedence. *This thought is stupid,* said Shai. *It makes no sense. These drums don't exist. I'm dead. I'm traveling between the regions of life and the Beyond. I'm in twilight: time retreats, it pulls away like . . . like the slow, dark beat of these drums, that only exist in my dying dream. . . .*

When the pain came, hard and bone-crushing, Shai told himself that he was still alive. For the dead, as everyone knows, feel nothing. He remembered that there had been an ambush.

Something hit him in the ribs and he groaned in misery.

"Ah, that's good," said a cold, deep voice. "The insect who fancies himself of the race of lords is coming to. He has a stubborn desire to live, but that doesn't mean that he'll have much chance at it."

That voice. . . .

Shai regretted now that he was not dead. Death would have been sweet and good and honorable. It would have shielded him from all the ebbs and swells of fortune. That voice!

"Good, let's help him. Throw a little cold water on him, that'll bring him around."

Icy needles clawed his face and he knew that he had to open his eyes sooner or later, stop playing at this farce. Dmitri Vashar looked very like the image which was graven in his memory. Armored, gloved in night, eyes shining in his most malevolent humor, he towered over Shai.

"Everything comes to him who knows how to wait," he said. "And the Great Serpent knows that I've waited. The farce is ended, young Shai. Or nearly so. I've decided, you see, that it will end by all the rules of the art. Don't look at me with that slack-jawed expression: I hope you understand what I'm telling you now."

Slowly Shai shook his head. The eyes of Dmitri Vashar mesmerized him. Before the Great Dark Lord he lost all resource, he became again the young uncertain student, bound to a pitiless discipline. Years of liberty among the warriors of the horde were forgotten, even Bearface's visage lost itself in bloody confusion. As for Lsi's presence, she was no more than an ever-retreating dream. He was a shivering young squire, an apprentice who stammered his answers. He was no more than a handful of clay shaped by the great artificer of fear.

"I'm dead!" he cried.

"Soon." The voice of Dmitri Vashar was a rasping sound in the wind of death. "That you protest proves on the contrary that you are most truly alive." The gloved hands of the Tetrarch of Night descended toward Shai and half-lifted him in the flickering torchlight.

"Shaguenigah!"

Someone who resembled a dark beast rose between the light and the shadow, and Shai remembered the rumors which had run rife among the young apprentices: When Dmitri Vashar was still one of the most respected officers of the citadel, he had taken for his squire a sort of imbecile monster, half idiot, half fiend, perhaps taken in some sacked village, but a monster quite devoted to him. This half-beast was called Shaguenigah. In the language of the gypsy tribes which had vanished more than two decades ago that word meant something like Eatbelly. Shaguenigah was at once Dmitri Vashar's toy, confidant and executioner, who never left his lair save on the rarest occasions. Since Shai had never seen him with his own eyes, he had thought all the horrors that people told of Vashar's squire were grotesque exaggeration.

But surfacing in his ocean of dust, cold and hot in turns, he discovered at the side of Dmitri Vashar's sinister countenance, an unspeakably snouted, red-eyed face.

"Well, *friend*, look at this fine young man I've told you so much about, all during our journey."

It was night and the citadel was fallen; when Dorn had killed Lord Ion, the Master-at-arms. The knights of Dmitri Vashar had passed in a mass. Shaguenigah, under cover of darkness, had followed his master, shadowlike—an evil, inseparable shadow.

The monster was clad in an ample brown cloak, of which he had cast back the hood to reveal the craters and wrinkles of his nightmarish face. Shai groaned heavily, conscious of his vulnerability.

"I do really want to turn you over to my friend for a while to see just what he's capable of doing with you. All through our long, our very long quest for justice, I talked to him so often of your treason, of the things you dared do to your own people, of the base manner which you soiled the nest in which you become great and intelligent—too intelligent. I talked to him about that and other things too—and this brave Shaguenigah, this simple and rustic, this unswerving creature—has conceived a great desire to meet you. Vengeance, says the proverb, has to be savored slowly, even if one has—like me—a wrath that burns in him like a sulfurous fire."

The monster growled and his eyes flickered with restless fire. "You're right, master, you're right."

Shai could not know what the beast agreed to; but perhaps it had only one driving thought— to pay homage to the wisdom of Dmitri Vashar, who was in its eyes ultimate perfection.

"Soon," said the general, "I shall be the master of all this land and I shall unite it under my banner. The time of barbarism will be nothing more than a memory. You, and those who have become your people, will prostrate themselves before me and come to feed from my hand. Perhaps in my great patience, I shall let some of you live. Without slaves, masters would not be masters."

Shaguenigah leaned further forward and took Shai's face between his hairy hands. "Pretty boy," he said. "Master, you are too kind."

A great flood of blood began to beat in Shai's brain. *I haven't done all this for nothing,* he thought. *I haven't traveled half the world, I haven't escaped the marauders of the sea, I haven't talked with the woman called the grand duchess of Carniole ... for* nothing! *To fall*

*into the hands of this bandit, this malignant
creature, this. . . . To become the plaything of
this beast, the toy of this animal!*

"Pretty, pretty boy," the monster repeated
complacently, and Shai understood in terror to
what ignominious fate Dmitri Vashar had con-
demned him. Shaguenigah's fingers slid into
Shai's hair in a long and hideous caress.

Shai drew away, succeeded in taking a less
humiliating posture. "Dmitri Vashar," he cried,
"listen to me!"

The great dark man shook his head slowly,
his eyes slitted, mouth compressed to a thin
straight wound in his pallid face. "What have
you left to say to me? Your words can't tell me
anything. What you have to say is what a
traitor would say."

"Dmitri Vashar! I regret nothing! What I
have done I *had* to do! And I would do it again,
I swear to you that I would do it again! And I
make you another promise: if I get out of here
alive I'll kill you!"

The general smiled slowly, with, it seemed,
circumspection. Then: "It's really a pity," he
said, "that you're not one of our own. So much
energy could have been used to better advantage. Aye, truly a pity. But there's no time
now to play at diversion. We have great things
afoot, my dear Shai, in which you still have a
role to play, a rather brief role, without effect,

without honor, but a role all the same. You talk about killing me. In your delirium you fling yourself about in every direction, like a poor beast trying to find its way out of an unbelievable labyrinth. My poor, charming boy—if you only knew...."

Dmitri Vashar lifted his supple, metal-studded hand and slapped Shai in the face. "You're going to learn one last lesson, a terrible but essential lesson. And when you've learned it, I'll let you ride at my side, into battle. Unfortunately you're not going to survive our victory."

The suffering was complex.

Physical first, because of the cold and the bonds which bit cruelly into his flesh. And spiritual, because of the uncertainty, because of the silence and the humiliation, because of the solitude and the fear.

The suffering was constant. It dug all its claws into his flesh and his soul.

He had quickly lost all sense of time. In a few hours, perhaps, when he had been dragged through Dmitri Vashar's camp, half running, half falling, most often carried in Shaguenigah's bosom. "It's the traitor," cried Dmitri Vashar's warriors. "It's Shai! He sold out the fortress of Bash and he blasphemed most grievously against the Great Serpent!"

Gibes poured from among the ranks of the

fanatical soldiers, and only their general's strict orders stopped them from tearing the unfortunate youth to pieces.

Bound to Shaguenigah's saddle, Shai had made the rounds of the camp, covered with railery and mud, his eyes streaming tears, his ears filled with a deafening thunder of voices.

Then everything had grown confused, nothing had mattered any longer.

A century later, in the strange creature's tent, he had fallen into a sleep so deep and so painful at once that he had lost all memory of it.

He dreamed, perhaps, but as a beast dreams, and when he regained awareness he had forgotten every image from the darkness.

Shaguenigah took pleasure in mistreating him, in savagely abusing him, mingling his sarcasm with obscene threats.

Always chained, and chained in such a way the least sudden move drew from him moans and cries, he very quickly acquired the habit of moving like a restless animal, half sliding, half crawling.

Sometimes, and these were the truly awful times, the most humiliating and painful, the monster took it into his head to care for Shai's person. He rubbed at the young man's body with a soiled scarf, rubbing his wounds raw, delaying, with a cruel and vacant smile, on his lower back and his genitals. He uttered all kinds of oaths and blasphemies and mindless ravings.

This slave among slaves, this ghost among ghosts had never had such a prey to himself, to humiliate, to drag about far and wide, like a flesh-and-blood plaything.

Sometimes too when Shai was not too exhausted by the long sessions of torture, Shaguenigah began to dance and sing, accompanying himself on the harp. He played admirably well, with a very sure instinct, and when he would thunder out an old marching song, a war song, a love song, he shed for a moment his monstrous monk's habit and became a bard, a troubador. Even his voice, ordinarily so ugly and rasping, discovered melodious inflexions which touched heart and soul. Then, for a moment, Shai recovered his courage, forgot that he was a slave whose wrists and ankles were long scarred from bonds of leather and metal, and tears of joy ran on his dirty face. But this dream usually lasted only for a very brief time. When he had finished his song, Shaguenigah became again the perverse and cruel creature he was, the vicious overseer who took pleasure in metamorphosing his captive, body and soul.

Shai seldom spoke, for he was not allowed to open his mouth without his master's permission, and then only to answer questions.

At first he had tried to escape, but each time Shaguenigah had given him to understand that he had to stay in his *place*. And his place was in the mud, like the dogs.

If he was mistreated on the least excuse, if he was spared no humiliation, at least he was fed regularly. He received a daily ration of meat and fat, of dried beans and even dried fruit. The water he had to drink was sometimes mixed with vinegar, but most often with red wine. It was not uncommon that he was allowed to drink his fill of a slightly sour beer. All this nourishment and all this drink kept him in relative good health.

One day when, in the grip of misery, he refused to eat and drink, Shag worked himself into a truly hideous rage, leaping from one foot to the other, threatening him and frothing at the mouth. "Eat!" he said, "and drink! You have to last till the day of the battle! The master won't have you to die before your time! Eat!"

And, eyes glittering with rage, the monster had fed Shai by force, like a bird destined for the butcher's knife.

It happened rarely that Shai dreamed. He was already far, far beyond the limits of his nerves. At least he thought so when the demon dragged him about by leash and collar. But one night, when he lay in Shaguenigah's tent, chained hand and foot to the centerpole, a dream slipped into his mind. . . .

(He was sitting on a high rock, in the very center of a gray desert. Harp music played, sad and far away. He was depressed and defeated and heavy chains weighted his ankles and his wrists. A strange sun shed an eye-hurting light over the landscape. In this light moved the still-vague figures of two riders. They neared him at a gentle trot, and he had the impression that the hooves of the horses, one black, one white, scarcely touched the ground. A ground which appeared sandy, without any rocks at all, without the thinnest sprig of grass. When the riders were near enough for him to see their faces he recognized Lsi and Bearface. They had both of them a look of misfortune. Their eyes rested on him in a sort of painful daze. They were dressed as if they were on a long journey, and Bearface wore all the insignia of his chieftainship as well as his favorite weapons. As for Lsi, she appeared broken with weariness and, strangely, kept her right hand on the butt of a blaster, the barrel of which was thrust through the massive silver-buckled belt she wore.

("It's time for battle, Shai," the hetman said soberly. "We've hunted everywhere. Where have you been?"

(The young woman echoed her companion.

"Yes, we've been looking everywhere for you and you never answered our calls. And now Bearface and I have put the strength of both our minds together to reach you.")

He waked with a start and began to weep. The tears did him good, brought him to the surface of his consciousness. He gathered himself up as far as he could against the centerpole, eager to breathe the nightwind; but soon the pain that had ebbed for a while came back into his limbs and he stayed unmoving in the dark to reassess the implications of his dream. A flood of hate welled up in his heart, ravaged his mind. Right then he would have tried to get up, to strike Shaguenigah as he slept a little distance away, buried under a heap of furs, but his strength betrayed him and he sank down in the dark again.

The same night, when he could not recover his sleep, the monster got up noisily, crossed the width of the tent from which he had drawn back the leather curtains, letting in a little wind and a little starry sky. That lasted only a moment before the wind and the stars were again sunk in the void. Shai heard Shaguenigah piss long and loudly. With satisfied grunts. Eatbelly came back into the tent. For a brief moment while the flap stayed up, Shai saw the brightness of the stars again and in an ephermeral flash, a blue light breaking into orange droplets.

In passing, without the slightest apparent reason, Shag kicked him. "I know you're not asleep," he said. "I know. But if you think you can get away ... haha ... you've gone completely crazy."

Shai, in spite of his suffering, felt himself less humble, less vulnerable. That light had reminded him that the world did not yet belong to Dmitri Vashar.

Strange blue ships coursed the sky.

Someday, if I survive the battle, I'll know more about these blue ships.

Eatbelly chuckled in the dark.

The next day, Shag led Shai in a promenade around the camp.

There was an agitation in the camp that the young man found curious. The soldiers did not waste time insulting him: they had, it seemed, other things to do.

"Hahahah," the brute said. "Fight, hard fight. You know, our folk fight their folk. Hard fight. Sure, our folk won."

Pain constricted Shai's throat. He felt his heart beat very hard.

"See," said Shag, "look, boy!"

Proudly the brute drew aside the folds of his cloak, revealing the large leather belt where he usually kept a collection of obscene trinkets and from which hung a long dagger, sheathed in red velvet. Passed through his belt, Shai recognized his blaster. The one that had been taken from him in his capture in the cursed canyon.

"Lord Vashar is very happy to see me dress nice, boy. So he gave me this. He said it was yours. It's mine now, because you, huhn, you don't need it no more. Right?"

Shai nodded as if he docilely, humbly approved what Eatbelly said.

Riders passed, spattering them with mud.

The sky was gray. Oppressive. With thick clouds which hid the sun. Brutally Shag hauled on the collar that circled Shai's neck to make him go faster.

"Good day," said the monster with no particular reason. "A day for war and massacre. Blood in the air. Smell the blood."

Shai sniffed as if he breathed deeply.

"Smell it?"

"Yes."

IX

THE DEATH OF THE BEAR

Each time he went outdoors like that, dragged about by Shag afoot or from his horse, Shai was painfully suspended between dread and resignation. But today his mind stayed clear and alert. He realized perfectly well what was going on around him, learned not without disquiet the size of the enemy camp. Superior in number, the enemy was evidently not; but its equipment and its weapons were far greater in sophistication and effectiveness than those the nomads had.

A few blasters more or less, the young man thought, *won't tilt the balance much. The hetman is in a trap. He'll fight with all the strength and courage a bear has, but he'll fall.*

Whole companies of infantry had fallen out for drill on a vast field. They looked formidable, these warriors, formidable and determined. Machines who would not flinch when Dmitri Vashar led them into battle.

Shaguenigah was not wrong. There was in this day's gray wind a smell of scarlet, an odor of blood and defeat.

The officers kept themselves apart, faces somewhat gloomy, while the sergeants, with great shouts, kept the companies at their drill.

A few taunts greeted Shai's passage, but they lacked conviction.

Near the enclosure, a very temporary enclosure which showed quite clearly that Dmitri Vashar's army had no intention to remain long in this vicinity, in a place battered by the wind, there was a gathering of ragged tents which afforded its inhabitants shelter in varying degrees from the rigors of the season.

It was to this place that Eatbelly dragged his prisoner, leading him roughly and sparing him neither commentary nor blows.

A group of frightened or at least cold-petrified creatures met Shaguenigah with somewhat stupid mimery, feigning in a certain confusion that they were pleased the monster had paid them this unseasonal visit.

These men and women were prisoners, spared

to serve as menial labor but also as recipients of the sexual urges of the soldiery.

After having ordered Shai to sit down and *don't budge from there*, Shaguenigah began to make overtures to the women of the tribe. He babbled and grimaced obscure compliments, going even so far as to sing to them, without the help of his harp, an old and slightly bawdy lovesong. When he had finished, he cast a look at a girl who might have been desirable enough if she were not covered with grease.

"Pretty young woman!" Shag cried, "if you be nice and make me happy, I'll make you a gift. I'll bring you meat and wine and you can fill your pretty guts!"

The brute was excited. The coming of battle had wakened his sexual instincts, and his eyes shone when he looked at Shai. "Wicked tongues say Shag doesn't do it 'cept with young boys but you're going to see that's not so. Come on, come on, girlie, come play with good old Shaguenigah!" From under his cloak he drew a gourd of liquor and showed it all about, chuckling. "When I do it with the little girl we drink."

Docile, the girl came near, already raising her skirts. She was long accustomed to submitting to the rough assaults of the soldiers. Her legs seemed to fascinate Shag, who began to undo his belt, without the least concern for what was going on around him. Shai saw the folk of the tribe make a circle around Shag and the girl: their entertainments were not very numerous and what was going to happen between Shag and the young captive could at least pass for an entertainment.

Shai stayed seated on his heels, exactly as his lord and master had ordered him, but he had seen the belt fall to the ground with the dagger and the blaster. *Fool*, Shai thought, *you poor old fool.*

The girl had lain down on her back, legs apart. Propping herself up on her elbows, she smiled rather vacantly while the *poor old fool* took up the position. Puffing up his chest he hastened to demonstrate his virility which was as evident as that of a stag. For food and wine, the involuntary prostitute would have received the homage of the Great God Pan himself and not whimpered.

Shag got down between the girl's thighs and Shai, sure that the act would not last long at all, wasted not a second.

He got up, his leash trailing grotesquely on the ground, and shoved one or two of the spectators; snatched up the blaster. Engrossed in his business, Eatbelly had not noticed a thing. He groaned mightily and rode his forced partner with cries of rage. At the moment when he began to afflict the girl with vividly imagined injuries, a groan went through the semicircle of spectators and they raised a mournful whisper. Shaguenigah's head transformed itself into a glowing gourd while the morning air filled with the hideous smell of burned meat. Eatbelly did not scream: he had no time: he died before he knew what had happened to him. When she saw the almost acephalic thing which held her in its embrace the girl, hardened as she was, started howling, backed by the chorus from the tribe.

Shai, thoroughly glad his legs were not chained, began to run toward the camp barricade. A guard tried to get into his path, but he struck him down without stopping.

The ease with which he succeeded in slipping out of the camp unapprehended surprised him; and he wondered, standing on the snow-flecked mud, panting, his chest burning and his mouth fouled with the taste of vomit, whether it was not all some ugly trick, whether a band of riders was not going to rush out to bring him back to Dmitri Vashar.

He reached the cover of the forest and toward noon, he killed two mounted patrolmen who came from their cover into an icy clearing.

He rode the low roads, used all the tricks of the terrain to hide himself from the pursuit he knew would come. During a brief rest he had succeeded in getting rid of his manacles, or more precisely, or breaking the chain that joined the two metal and leather cuffs. He rode then more at ease, still trailing his leash behind him. At the first chance he used his blaster to burn off the leather strap which reminded him of those unspeakable hours.

When he fell upon a friendly squadron, Shai burst into tears. The warriors let him weep without uttering a word, then gave him food and drink.

"The hetman thought you were dead," said the patrol commander. "That was a terrible blow to him."

"I've come from the enemy camp," Shai said. "Look at the chains and the collar. They treated me like an animal. And there are a lot of them, an awful lot. As for their weaponry—it's far better than ours."

The patrol chief nodded his head sadly. "We know a bit about that. Alas, the first battle was a few days ago. We were able to push the assault back, but at a price. Kjul died in that battle."

"Kjul!"

Brave, faithful Kjul. Another page had been turned.

"And you don't know all of it, Shai. You don't know all of it."

A painful knot swelled in the young man's throat.

"The hetman was wounded. Nothing fatal, but all the same. . . . It hasn't helped us. I'm doubly glad to get you back. Having you back is going to be like a second birth for Bearface. Gods be with you, Shai!"

"My son! You're alive!" The hetman crushed the young man in his arms. There was as much of force as of tenderness in his embrace but Shai, who knew his protector well, understood that it was out of despair. "Getting you back gives me strength," he said. "Without you, I was only a very old animal, my son, and I didn't know if I could keep on fighting or whether I ought to lie down at the depth of my den. When the dark of winter comes, Shai, bears try to find a quiet place to sleep . . . If I hadn't had Lsi with me—"

"Don't talk like that, father," Shai said. "How would your people go on fighting without you?"

"My people know that all men are mortal and replaceable. To worship a chief like a god is a great mistake. Worship like that has caused the fall of whole civilizations. I'm losing my power now, Shai, and I know too that my end is near. In the great battle ahead we shall lose many of our illusions and almost all our certitudes. If we come out of that fight the victors we shall have to take the fate of the people in our hands. Surround yourself with intelligent men and try to continue what we've begun—"

Then they sat down around a low table and the servants brought them beer, roast meat and dried fruit. They ate in silence, all three of them, trying in the depths of their hearts to find reason to rejoice and to hope.

"I saw an omen in the sky," Shai said, after a while. "A blue light, with orange edges. I tell you we're being watched by the people in space. But they won't intervene in these fights which involve the civilizations of the earth. They're content to watch us, like strange beasts. They aren't worth much more than the Oligarchs of the fortresses are."

"Why do you talk to us about them? What do you think they would do for us, these poor exiles? They're nothing more than ghosts. We at least have a reason to go on living, to go on fighting. Even despair isn't really the end of us."

They parted a little later. When Shai and Lsi were back in their tent they waited long moments before touching each other, before talking, before their bodies came together again.

(When he fell asleep, Shai fell into a terrible dream. He watched Bearface die. A quick death, without glory.)

* * *

The patrols who came in at more or less regular intervals to make their report, told of a major troop movement and Bearface immediately ordered his various regiments to make contact. A hit and run tactic would let the rest of the army prepare itself for the shock of the oncoming regiments.

A chill wind swept the scantly risen sun.

Bearface and Shai quitted the camp under a pale sun that held a disquieting red taint. The oriflammes and standards cracked with fury as if to speak to them in encouragement. The earth shook under the hooves of the horses as at the coming of an earthquake.

Clouds which took on the shapes of monstrous beasts or vast swollen balloons of poisonous gas floated in the sky, in the grip of the chill winds.

The shock of the two armies was terrible.

The combat at once showed itself merciless. There could be but one conclusion to the two-sided engagement: the annihilation of one or the other.

Formidable apparition, Dmitri Vashar galloped at the head of his cavalry, among his liegemen and his knights.

In his right hand, in a glove reinforced with flexible metal, he had a sort of studded wooden club with which he performed dire prodigies.

When the two lines met, the general knifed into the opposing ranks like the ram of a ship in a stormy sea. A bloody wine spattered the dulled sun.

Bearface who fought as furiously as his implacable enemy attempted more than once to get face to face with Dmitri Vashar in the midst of the battle. He told himself by all the traditions of the men of the plain and the forest that if he succeeded in defying him, in striking him a mortal blow, he would make such a disturbance in the opposing ranks that the fortunes of war might turn in his favor. But the knights of Dmitri Vashar were vigilant; they managed to surround their general with an unassailable defense.

The slaughter was terrible. The savagery of the battle touched by tenacious rancor, by a hate which legend or lies had patiently fostered, soon peaked in horror, in almost ecstatic fervor. It was the great red banquet of war.

Toward the evening of that battle, when the carnage had reached apogee, a group of enemy horsemen surrounded the hetman and succeeded in separating him from his lieutenants.

He who had desired with all his might to gain a single combat, some saving duel of chieftains, only managed to fall into a stupid trap.

The hetman realized quickly that he had

gotten ahead of his forces. For in the heat of battle, one of his wounds had reopened. Now in a red fog shot through with glittering illusion he saw coming toward him the bloody faces of enemy riders. He defended himself as best he could, striking and parrying, wielding his axe with as much advantage of experience as of strength. The vigor of his blows diminished. The red night crept about him, while his axe did its somber duty.

The enemies who had thus ensnared him must retreat three times before one of them, coming at the hetman from the back, succeeding in getting in a brutal blow. A furious growl rose in the bear's chest. But it was a cry of agony which passed his lips. Still clutching his battle axe he pitched from the stirrups with a majestic slowness.

When Bearface's riders finally succeeded in breaking that fatal encirclement they were too late.

Their chief lay in the bloodied mud, trampled by hundreds of hooves. His skull had been split and broken.

Dorn the dwarf gave a dark wail which froze his companions' blood. On his ravaged face tears mixed in the red blood of war.

The battle was lost.

* * *

Shai was mad with rage.

He no longer understood the orders of battle. At the beginning, strictly, he had followed Bearface's orders which had put him in a reserve force.

When they brought him alarming news he had wanted to get out there and throw himself into the mêlée. But the officers had at once persuaded him against that. He must await the hetman's orders, for the hetman must lead them to victory or at least save them from great defeat.

Now the hetman was out of reach, the orders no longer came, save shapeless, incomprehensible instruction, and a dire premonition seized Shai's heart.

Shai was mad with rage.

A confused thought, a red thought came to batter itself against the barricades of his mind. A thought which came out of the heart of the battle.

His hands clenched while the message thrust into his brain. He knew that it was Bearface's farewell and that the battle had turned decisively against them.

He raised his hand as if to hurl a final wave into the assault, but the officers above him averted their eyes.

The red and burning impulse died. Stopped cold.

Parenthesis V

THE HANGING GARDENS OF FARAWAY

The two lovers walked beneath the artificial sun of the orbital station.

The woman said: "I don't know why, but I have the feeling that something's changed. Maybe we've ... succeeded this time. Maybe we've been ... heard."

The man shook his head and smiled sadly. "Heard—by whom?"

And he added: "There's no one in this night to hear us. Everything's dead. We're sterile. Soon it'll all be over. We'll have gone, in silence—"

"You're wrong to talk like that," she said. "Something isn't the way it was, I feel it."

"We'll see," he sighed.

In an alley of the park they found a body. A man who was still young had chosen this place to end his life—for they had no crime on Faraway.

She turned her head. "He was wrong to do that," she murmured. "That's not the solution."

He gave a joyless laugh. "For him, it was."

Then they walked toward the hanging gardens.

They were having a party there.

X

TOWARD NEW SHORES

Shai slept against Lsi's side at the midst of their embarkation, while Dorn surveyed with a sullen eye the fisherman and his son who managed the masted bark. The rigging, quite filled with the stinging cold wind, groaned gently.

Shai at the depth of his dreams, struggled in vain against the return of dark memories.

Lsi's hand gently rested against the young man's shoulder. Lsi was not asleep. She mulled things over in a sort of hebetude, her head filled with a kaleidoscope of violent images. Women and children running, men trying to organize resistance inside the fortified camp. Sudden flames had burst into the sky, befouling the clouds. Flames which heralded the death of hope in a burning without a tomorrow. She had started to run, even she, but it was in search of a horse, a weapon—

Then she had seen Shai, at the head of a decimated troop that came through the gates and—it was all lost in the smoke, in the tumult, in the chaos of defeat.

Dmitri Vashar's anger remained. He was cheated of a part of his victory.

When they had brought him the head of Bearface, all besmirched with blood, he had burst into savage laughter, but a laughter at length bereft of joy. Then when an officer had come to report to him that Shai could not be found among the living or among the dead, he had felt a little bit of ice slide down his neck while a fiery serpent writhed and coiled in his bowels.

"The nest is not destroyed!" he cried. "The teeth of the dragon might be sown even in the depths of winter cold. And this winter is only beginning!"

The officer who had brought Dmitri Vashar the news of this disappointment bowed deeply as if to leave. Doing so he respectfully presented his naked, shaven nape, for he held his helm clutched in his right arm as military etiquette demanded. He exposed himself thus in a sort of unconscious humility.

Abruptly the general shot out his gloved hand, the terrible right hand which lacked two fingers but which was capable of breaking and tearing. And this hand which held the heavy warclub struck as the serpent strikes.

Under the violence of the blow the officer's skull shattered. The fearful weapon had killed the bearer of bad news outright. The messenger fell heavily, without a cry.

Died without knowing what had hit him.

"I want," said Dmitri Vashar, "someone to find this young Shai. Dead or alive. But preferably alive."

Then he wrapped himself in his cloak as if he had suddenly become aware of the cold.

"Shag. Poor bastard. Stupid, lousy animal. For a greasy female you let slip him who will sow the Dragon's Teeth. If I could get my hands on you now, poor fool, I'd curse you."

Later the general had a captive shaman brought to his tent and brutally bade him kneel at his feet. "Hear me well, whoreson, for I don't want my meaning to escape you. You see this disgusting trophy? This head of a beast we cut off in the battle? You do know it, yes. *You recognize it, don't you? Say so!*"

"Yes," said the shaman in a trembling voice.

"I recognize it. It's the head of the hetman. I never liked him."

"I'm delighted to hear you say that, you poor crawling worm. They said so, and I have thought, I have to think that you know simple things quite well, even the thousand and one ways to preserve things, to embalm things, to make human flesh survive beyond the cruelest death. I want you to see to it that this head is not touched by corruption, that it becomes the symbol of my victory. Our enemies will say of me: 'That's Dmitri Vashar, who defeated Bearface!' " And the general added coldly: "If you fail in that task I'll have you boiled alive."

The shaman, who had understood quite well, assured the great Dmitri Vashar of his devotion and his abasement. "All my thoughts will be faithful to you," he vowed cautiously, bowing to the earth. Then he fled, almost crawling, to get to his cauldrons and his potions.

Shai did not escape his dream. It was like wading endlessly in a swamp or a wide pond, not deep, to be sure, but it stretched as far as the eye could see.

Shai kept seeing the last stage of the battle again and again. The atrocity of their defeat.

There was death in his soul.

(He had fled with Lsi, with Dorn urging them on, the fortified camp in the grip of panic.)

Death! It had come. It had the face of Dmitri Vashar. Set on the crest of a wave, set at the height of a rocky cliff—insinuating itself into the gaps of his consciousness.

Dorn gazed at the two men, father and son, and Lsi dared not move, for fear of waking Shai.

And in Shai's dream they were there again. All the people in the drama. The protagonists as well as the bit players.

They moved.

They cried aloud.

They commanded.

They broke into mirth. They burst, red flowerings like blood.

They rode.

They sang.

They prayed to gods both old and new.

They howled at death. Or they cried for mercy.

They fornicated. They reproduced. Or they were sterile instead.

They conspired. Schemed. Connived.

But all, all were there: protagonists and bit players.

"Watch yourselves," said Dorn, "for I don't trust the rest of you. One false movement and I'll fry you."

"But, lord," pleaded the old fisherman who

held the rudder, while his son took care of the sail, "I have no reason to betray you, you and yours. I'm a sworn enemy of the shamans (may the sea crabs feed on their entrails!) and you don't need to threaten me. I'll do whatever you ask me to, I'll go wherever you tell me to— We're poor dogs, robbed by the shamans, held to ransom by the pirates— And now there are thousands of soldiers falling upon us!"

"Shut up! You're babbling!" In Dorn's hand the blaster was a malefic beast, ready to bite with all its gleaming teeth.

"Those are terrible weapons," said the old sailor in a thin voice, "but at the end of things they aren't worth much."

"What do you mean, you poor fool, you lousy idiot, what do you mean they're not worth much? You louse-ridden old goat!"

"Yes, lord, and you can insult me as much as you like, it won't change anything. Kill me with that terrible weapon, kill my son too. You're going to go to the bottom along with your two friends. You'll die, you'll die! With or without that weapon—"

"I haven't got the time to argue with you, you poor dog," Dorn cried. "I just want you to do what I tell you."

The old man nodded. "I'll obey you, for such has always been my intention. Where do you want to go with your friends, lord?"

"How should I know? The only thing I can tell you is that Vashar's hunting dogs can't swim in this cold water and in a boat we can win a little time. That's why I've asked you to get out to sea. Later we'll see—"

"We *are* out to sea, lord. At the mercy of the wind, at the mercy of the pirates. You can be sure that the carrion birds are already flying and they'll come, into the bosom of the conquerors, to take all they can take—"

"Later there'll be nothing to do but go back to the coast and skim the shore a little. You're an experienced sailor, you know what you have to do."

"If the shamans get wind of your flight they'll count it a pleasure and a sacred duty to tell everything they know to the general's hunters. I'm risking my skin and my son's in this business. But, like I said, your hetman was good to us, for a while. He even tried to change things."

"Yes, he tried. Fate's harlot, he did try. And he died doing it."

"Not so, lord, not so. He died because his time had come."

"Imbecile. Let's hope the shamans don't know what we're doing. They hated the hetman beyond all reason."

Silence fell between the two men, leaving

the last word to the sea. A sea gray and noisy, under a leaden sky. A storm sky.

Dunja IV, grand duchess of Carniole, was home again. In sight of her own lands. The river shone majestically under the winter sun. Perhaps it was snowing there, in the heart of the land.

An escort awaited her on shore, to accompany her to the silent, sorrowful ruins of Mahagonny.

While captain Otman's men were busied at docking maneuvers, Dunja leaned on the railing and began to dream like a little girl. Confused feelings, indefinible, warred in her. *I grow young again,* she thought. *I grow young because of that boy. Never trust old volcanoes, the proverb says.*

Then as ever, when she returned from one of her voyages, the grand duchess saw the janissaries of her escort draw near to the debarkation point. The officer in command took off his golden helmet and cried: "God save your Grace! Have you had a good voyage?"

"I can't complain," replied the grand duchess. "But we did meet a few surprises, Captain Otman and I. And you, Cottian, are you satisfied with the turn of events?"

"Nothing to report, your Grace, if you don't

count the abortive invasions of the poor uncurables."

"Oh, always the same thing, we have to reinforce the patrols. And aside from that?"

"Your dog Kayyam mounted your bitch Pineda. Good news, isn't it, your Grace?"

"Certainly, Lieutenant Cottian. Thank you. It's quite rare these days."

The janissary officer bowed ceremoniously. Dunja IV smiled: she loved this handsome gangling man, who was ready for love and war, like all the janissaries of her personal guard. She made a redoubtable consummation of these warriors of luxury.

She reflected that she had been long delayed in her return to her subterranean palace at Mahagonny. Among her faithful dogs and her attentive janissaries. But a touch of melancholy mingled with her impatience. She prepared to go out on land. Suddenly she shivered. What—or whom—dammit, was she thinking of?

"Fine day for the season," Lt. Cottian said a little while later, gallantly offering her the support of his arm. "But they never last."

Of course he was right, weather never made her shiver like that. Dunja IV, grand duchess of Carniole, said to her officer: "The car, waste no time; I want to be back among my furnishings—"

The armored electric vehicle, large as a moving house, awaited them. It looked like a great placid tapir. It was an automobile maintained with care and furnished with modern defensive weapons. When she was inside one of these mechanical monsters Dunja felt that she had penetrated into a kind of shelter where nothing grievous could befall her.

When the grand duchess was seated inside the giant tank, comfortably upholstered so as not to give it too military a feeling, it was in such poetic and civil terms that Cottian presented things . . . Only when the grand duchess had taken her place did the men of her escort take their places again.

"Cigarette?" inquired the officer.

"Thank you, my friend," said the grand duchess, her eyes slitted.

The vehicle began to move toward Mahagonny.

The waves grew rougher. Soon they came over the gunwale of the little craft.

Dorn who had begun to drowse, the blaster trembling slightly in his chilled hand, jumped violently. "Son of a bitch!" he yelled. And tried to stand up in the boat. "I'll kill you!"

Lsi, who had also given way to sleep, waked as abruptly. Stood up with dagger in hand.

"Don't worry," said the old sailor, "there's no

trick to fear. It's the storm that's coming. Yes, it's coming, and you can't do anything about it."

Shai too, now that the noise had drawn him from his web of dreams, tried to catch his balance. "Where are we?" His voice shook with absurd quaverings. Sleep had made him several years younger, lent him an almost transparent look.

"We're going to die," Lsi said. "Maybe that's better."

The old sailor's son, who had kept himself in a kind of prudent reserve, suddenly decided to intervene. "No one's going to die."

Dorn turned his anger toward the young man. "Shut up. Or I'll put a hole in you! I'll put a hole in you right in front of your father's eyes." The laser's black eye was trained on the sailor's groin.

"Oh? You put a hole in me, lord, and like my father says, pretty quick you'll have a hole of your own."

Shai came to himself all at once. "Dorn! Talk of killing— Let him talk. He knows a lot of things you and I don't know. Like how to get out of this!"

He pointed skyward. Even in the brief passage of time in which the argument had started, it had grown charcoal-gray.

"Shit!" Dorn looked at the clouds that raced

like wild horses. His face showed an unbounded anguish.

"That's the way of it," the old fisherman said soberly. "We're in the storm season."

Dunja IV, grand duchess of Carniole, was very glad to find herself once more in her usual environment, with her books, her cassettes, her favorite pets. But she was strangely unable to relax entirely, and to calm her jangled nerves she convoked her administrative council without further delay.

Her confidante the fair Natasha Navashyne formally advised her against working so early in the day and prescribed for her several hours of sleep in which to recover; but Dunja walked out. She needed to argue with the men and women of her administrative council instead of slipping into the abyss of sterile sleep. She dressed carefully in a shining but very masculine suit and without listening to Ms. Navashyne's objections, headed for the council hall.

In the corridors of the underground palace, people came and went almost furtively. People who greeted her with respect, people many of whom carried upon their faces the terrible glittering marks.

Natasha Navashyne walked behind Dunja IV.

Unhappily. She found her mistress (and

friend) changed for the worse. *As if wrapped up within herself.*

Poor Dunja.

Natasha Navashyne, who had enough ambition for any four human beings, felt with all her intelligence and instincts that something had just slipped into the gears of the great well-oiled machine. But what, yes—hell, what?

In front of the council room the guards presented arms and courtesies to their grand duchess; then the doors opened without the least sound.

Everyone was already there.

For Dunja IV hated to be kept waiting.

Natasha Navashyne gave a long sigh as she listened to her mistress run roughshod over her most eminent advisors and most expert coworkers.

"We have to change our plans," said the grand duchess.

That produced a confused but decidedly disapproving murmur, as if her Grace had just proposed an obscenity.

"I think I expressed myself clearly. Anyhow, I don't see anything else to do. For too long, following agreements several decades out of date, we've all held ourselves apart from what goes on in the outside world."

A hand went up to claim the floor.

It belonged to Colonel Turckman.

"Yes?"

"I've always respected your decisions, madam. You know that."

"I know it," the grand duchess said coldly. "Go on."

"I fear I don't understand you any longer."

"That's a pity, colonel. A man of your valor and intelligence ought to pick things up in midword."

"But, madam, saving your Grace, I do understand you only too well! You're about to let your emotions sway your good sense—"

There was an unaccustomed stirring in the council room.

Natasha Navashyne twitched. If the colonel was onto it, if he had noticed the change that had come over the grand duchess—then truly something had gotten into the works. And it was important that all the machinery worked flawlessly.

"My friend, I think what you say, in an excess of zeal and affection for my person, does get ahead of your good sense."

Natasha Navashyne blanched.

The administrative council—was it about to be shaken by a sudden storm? The words *palace coup* danced for a moment in fair Natasha's head.

Quite pale, the grand duchess was on her feet.

Her eyes flashed lightnings.

She's wrong not to listen to me. A few hours of sleep would have avoided this useless altercation with men as brilliant as Colonel Sabd Truckman. Can I repair matters?

"Please accept my apologies." The officer, against all intent, beat a retreat. But Natasha Navashyne knew that he was an excellent tactician.

"Gladly, colonel. I do accept them gladly. But my decision stands ... so far as I'm concerned. Perhaps, to accommodate everyone, we could vote a little later?"

Sabd Truckman bowed very slightly. For him the confrontation was finished.

Another hand lifted. That of Deonte Farquar of Alexandropol. In Mahagonny he represented spiritual authority. "Your suggestion is very wise," he said. "An immediate vote would only confuse things. Let us wait awhile. There's no hurry. Saying that, I remain, madam, your attentive servant."

Liar, Natasha thought.

Dmitri Vashar, with a squadron of light cavalry, galloped along the beach. The wind beat like an artery. The sea was barriered with a curtain of mist. It looked like the gray-green set of some vast theater.

Dmitri Vashar's hands seemed frozen upon the reins.

Cheated of his victory! He had had countless victims killed. He had waded in the blood of his enemies, but always there remained the fear of seeing the Dragon's Teeth sown.

Confusedly he felt his triumph slipping from him. Teeth clenched, he invoked the Great Serpent. All his cynicism fled him while he raised the storm winds.

Against the flank of his horse thumped a leathern sack. Still empty. But when the shaman had worked his magic, it would hold the embalmed head of his enemy. And one day— soon, he hoped—he would make a second one to hold Shai's head as well. Then he could, with nothing more to fear, gather the whole world under his banner. Things would fall back into order.

The Great Serpent would reign again over the citadels of the Faith.

Masters would be masters again.

Slaves would be slaves.

That was the way things ought to be. According to the terms of the ancient law.

(*When the great hurricane had come, the golden serpent which stands for law threw its sevenfold coils about the land of law and declared thus: "When the great storm has ceased, what is within must remain there, and what is*

without must be compelled to remain there."
And the serpent of the law having added no
other words to what he had said, his words
became law.)

The wind blew now with violence, and the
riders could advance but slowly along the misty
shore.

The hunt was no longer possible.

Besides, it obeyed nothing now but the laws
of chance.

. Soon it would be necessary to give up and
turn back.

Shai and the young harlot must have had a
great deal of outside help. Dmitri Vashar determined to put the survivors of the carnage to
the torture.

Then, much against his will, he gave the
signal to turn back.

The sea was no more than a shadow-play.

The waves constantly came at the gunwales of
the boat, and maneuvering it became almost
impossible.

Dorn, his eyes wild, felt the situation slipping his control. Nausea bent him double and
in his clenched fist the laser was no more than
a child's toy.

Shai helped the young sailor haul on the
sheets but the boat danced in the midst of the

wind-driven mist. Lsi bit her lips to stifle her cries. Terror was a leaden hand on the sea.

Suddenly they saw in the tearing of a vast curtain of mist a rugged, threatening coastline. There was a kind of inlet there, which looked like the very mouth of hell. They were headed straight for it.

"Old fool!" Dorn screamed over the crash of the storm, "you're going to kill us all!"

But the old fool just smiled. With just the edge of disdain. Bent over the tiller which shook like an insect's beak, he held their bow steady.

Meanwhile the two youths struggled with the sheets.

"Hold on tight," cried the sailor. "Pull as hard as you can!"

Shai did as he was told, his eyes filled with salt, his fingers slippery with blood.

There was sudden turbulence and as the boat began to slew about, taking the waves on its side, taking in the sea in sheets, Lsi yelled, sure that their boat was going to break up on a reef, but the rocks seemed to have vanished under a final surge, a last sounding flood—

The mist wrapped them about again in its gentle folds, but they drifted in calmer water now. Stony arms had closed behind them, protecting them from the fury of the storm.

The old sailor, without saying a word, brought

the boat to shore. They wallowed in a gloomy
little inlet.

"We're out of danger," the old man said.

"For now," Dorn chuckled, his hand still
clenched on his blaster, as if it were a luck
charm.

"Where are we?" Shai asked.

"On Moro Isle. It's separated from the coast
by some few miles of cold water. It's not
inhabited, though there are some odd rumors
about it. No one will come to look for you here.
At least not right away."

The three fugitives nodded. They understood
that they had a reprieve, a time to reflect.

"We can hold out here a few days," the sailor
said then. "Then you have to trust us again."

Shai leaned close to Lsi, took her in his arms.

In spite of the cold, the defeat, the storm, he
felt a strange warmth well up in his chest.

Something told him that somewhere, behind
that mist and that cold, prodigious changes
were in the offing. He thought he heard Bearface's disembodied voice echoing in the depths
of his heart.

"Come," he said to Lsi. "Let's go see our
island."

ENDPIECE

*The fingers on the electronic harp grew heavy, icy claws—nails of cold nacre. Frozen notes went out to meet the silence.

*The Crystal Desert echoed with unaccustomed sounds: like the distant beats of some diseased heart, come to the end of its rhythm.

*The harpist's eyes are sealed by the crystal sickness, and his mask is crossed with hideous cracks.

*It's all finished, he sings, but his voice hesitates, as if he is no longer sure of anything . . . His hands catch in the strings, sending northward notes which finally lose themselves in the gray void.

DAW

The really great fantasy books are published by DAW:

Andre Norton

☐ LORE OF THE WITCH WORLD   (#UE1750—$2.50)
☐ HORN CROWN   (#UE1635—$2.95)
☐ PERILOUS DREAMS   (#UE1749—$2.50)

C.J. Cherryh

☐ THE DREAMSTONE   (#UE1808—$2.75)
☐ THE TREE OF SWORDS AND JEWELS
    (#UE1850—$2.95)

Lin Carter

☐ DOWN TO A SUNLESS SEA   (#UE1937—$2.50)
☐ DRAGONROUGE   (#UE1982—$2.50)

M.A.R. Barker

☐ THE MAN OF GOLD   (#UE1940—$3.95)

Michael Shea

☐ NIFFT THE LEAN   (#UE1783—$2.95)
☐ THE COLOR OUT OF TIME   (#UE1954—$2.50)

B.W. Clough

☐ THE CRYSTAL CROWN   (#UE1922—$2.75)

NEW AMERICAN LIBRARY
P.O. Box 999, Bergenfield, New Jersey 07621

Please send me the DAW Books I have checked above. I am enclosing
$_____ (check or money order—no currency or C.O.D.'s).
Please include the list price plus $1.00 per order to cover handling costs.

Name _____

Address _____

City _____ State _____ Zip Code _____
Please allow at least 4 weeks for delivery